When she saw Luca waiting for her through the glass entrance of her apartment building, her pulse still reared and bucked like a skittish horse.

Dressed in a black suit, the breadth of his chest caused the lapels to pull open enough to hint at the power beneath but not make it look as if the suit was too small. A white shirt and black tie that disappeared beneath a suit jacket buttoned at lean hips. It should have screamed uniform, not boardroom, but there was something about the man that made him look *more*. Her gaze ran upwards, and she decided that it was his face.

His jawline was as sharp as his collar and, clean shaven, the morning sun glanced off angles that would make a supermodel weep. Dark waves were swept back neatly, shorter at the sides and longer on top, and not a single hair was out of place. Neat. Compact. Efficient. The large dark glasses hid his eyes, making him look inscrutable. Dispassionate even.

And *that* was what frustrated her. Luc's utterly professional behavior only made her wildly inappropriate reaction to him more obvious, she thought as she emerged from the apartment complex.

Hot Winter Escapes

Sun, snow and sexy seductions...

Whether it's a trip to the Swiss Alps or a rendezvous on a gorgeous Hawaiian beach, warming up in front of the fire or basking in the sizzling sun, these billion-dollar getaways provide the perfect backdrops for even more scorching winter romances and passionately-ever-afters!

Escape to some winter sun in...

Bound by Her Baby Revelation by Cathy Williams

An Heir Made in Hawaii by Emmy Grayson

Claimed by the Crown Prince by Abby Green

One Forbidden Night in Paradise by Louise Fuller

And get cozy in these luxurious snowy hideaways...

A Nine-Month Deal with Her Husband
by Joss Wood

Snowbound with the Irresistible Sicilian
by Maya Blake

Undoing His Innocent Enemy
by Heidi Rice

In Bed with Her Billionaire Bodyguard
by Pippa Roscoe

All available now!

Pippa Roscoe

IN BED WITH HER BILLIONAIRE BODYGUARD

HARLEQUIN
PRESENTS

ISBN-13: 978-1-335-59317-7

In Bed with Her Billionaire Bodyguard

Copyright © 2023 by Pippa Roscoe

For questions and comments about the quality of this book,
please contact us at CustomerService@Harlequin.com.

Harlequin Enterprises ULC
22 Adelaide St. West, 41st Floor
Toronto, Ontario M5H 4E3, Canada
www.Harlequin.com

Printed in U.S.A.

Recycling programs
for this product may
not exist in your area.

Pippa Roscoe lives in Norfolk near her family and makes daily promises to herself that this is the day she'll leave the computer to take a long walk in the countryside. She can't remember a time when she wasn't dreaming about handsome heroes and innocent heroines. Totally her mother's fault, of course—she gave Pippa her first romance to read at the age of seven! She is inconceivably happy that she gets to share those daydreams with you all. Follow her on Twitter, @pipparoscoe.

Books by Heidi Rice

Harlequin Presents

The Wife the Spaniard Never Forgot
His Jet-Set Nights with the Innocent

A Billion-Dollar Revenge

Expecting Her Enemy's Heir

The Diamond Inheritance

Terms of Their Costa Rican Temptation
From One Night to Desert Queen
The Greek Secret She Carries

The Royals of Svardia

Snowbound with His Forbidden Princess
Stolen from Her Royal Wedding
Claimed to Save His Crown

Visit the Author Profile page
at Harlequin.com for more titles.

This book is for Julie Chivers for reasons including, but not limited to:

- Answering random and overly complicated contract and copyright queries.

- Knitting in meetings.

- Sharing your fantastical reading journey.

- Supplying me with a carefully curated, and constant, stream of high quality TikTok videos.

- Unwittingly inspiring THIS WHOLE BOOK!

So thank you, Julie!
It's a pleasure being your friend.

PROLOGUE

LUCA CALVINO SAT trying not to stare at the man in the hospital bed attached to more monitors than Luca had seen in his entire life. That the man was Nate Harcourt, billionaire businessman and barely a few years from Luca's own age of thirty-three, was mildly disconcerting.

'It's not as bad as it looks.'

'It looks pretty bad,' Luca replied truthfully.

'It's not.'

'Okay.'

The private hospital in Switzerland was as luxurious as some of the finest hotels Luca had ever had the pleasure of staying in and the security was top-notch, as it should be. Large windows looked out onto a wintry forest fit for a fairy tale. Warm leather and wood accents decorated the room that might look like the lounge of some metropolitan apartment but hid almost half a million euros' worth of medical equipment to suit any emergency.

'Pegaso has a pretty impressive portfolio for such

a young company,' Nathanial Harcourt said, bringing his attention back to the matter at hand.

'Is ten years that young?' Luca enquired with a hint of sarcasm, disliking that he was only slightly rising to the Englishman's bait.

'It is when you have a family business that spans four hundred.'

'Fair point,' Luca conceded. Until a year ago, Nathanial Harcourt had been the rising star of the business world. He might have come from so much family money it reeked of established nepotism, had what he'd done with it not become legendary. But then he'd disappeared off the face of the planet—reportedly to go and find himself in Goa.

This was a far cry from Goa.

'Cancer?' he asked, curious as to what Nate would choose to tell him.

There was a moment; an appraisal between two dominant men.

'Aneurism. Cerebral.'

Luca nodded, unable to stop his eyebrows rising in surprise and reassessing the man in front of him. The upper part of the hospital bed was raised, across which hung a half table on a metal arm that was doing an excellent job of supporting what looked like an office's worth of paperwork and a laptop within Nate's reach.

'Pegaso's revenue was significant last year, not such an easy thing to do in today's economic climate. You have contracts through the majority of mainland Europe with several businesses, including this,' Nate stated, his hand opened to gesture to the hospital they were in—a discreet medical facility that employed the best of the best to those who needed the utmost privacy. Luca knew this because, as Nathanial had noted, Pegaso oversaw the security of the entire facility.

'I'm familiar with my CV.'

'But you haven't managed to break into any English-speaking markets.'

'It's funny,' Luca said with a gentle shoulder shrug, 'I would have thought that as a businessman who sits on three boards, is the CEO of two more, and is *very* high up in your own family business, you'd have a little more common sense than to alienate someone you are about to ask a favour from.'

'It's not a favour, it's an offer.'

The discreet monitor trilled sharply and Luca didn't miss the wince of pain and the jerk of Nate's hand as if he'd wanted to press it against his head, but wouldn't concede to such an open display of pain. Stubborn. Luca could respect that.

'Spill, before it's time for more meds,' Luca said.

'It's not as bad as it looks.'

'Keep telling yourself that.'

Nate managed a smirk and the beeping on the monitor settled again.

'I need you to protect my sister.'

Nate pointed at a folder on the half table and Luca stood to retrieve it. He had no problem verbally sparring with the English billionaire, but he had no intention of degrading the man by making him reach for it himself. A cerebral aneurism was no joke.

Luca opened the folder: Hope Harcourt, twin sister of Nathanial Harcourt, twenty-nine years old, single, Director of Marketing for Harcourts, the world's leading luxury department store. He sat back, looking at pictures of a blonde with delicate features. Although Hope and Nathanial Harcourt were twins, there was no more than a normal sibling similarity between them. His eyes grazed over high cheekbones and fine hair, working hard not to be distracted by the bolt of attraction that struck him hard. He purposely ignored the dark, espresso rich eyes that seemed to pick at his focus and pushed aside the pictures and bio, to pick up the press articles in the back.

More Than Just a Pretty Face? Hope Announced as Harcourts' Marketing Director.

Luca scanned the next few headlines for lesser or increasing degrees of offensive misogyny, unsurprised that the by-line bore the same name.

Harcourt Fiancé Reveals Socialite's Deep Insecurities.
Harcourts' Flawed Diamond! The Truth Behind the Breakup.

Luca rode out the familiar burn of resentment towards the tabloids who would take advantage of anything and anyone for a scoop. But he also understood that for every journalist there was someone ready and waiting to reap the rewards.

'My sister gets hit pieces like this all the time.'

'So why now?'

'Because I'm…here. I can't protect her.'

For the first time since meeting Nate Harcourt, the frustration was genuine, the anger palpable.

'You want Pegaso to protect her from the press?' She wouldn't be the first woman to court the press to advance her career, sales or reputation, Luca mused. 'What makes you think that she would even want it?'

'Because she's not like that and because something's coming. I don't know what. But the shareholders at Harcourts are being tight-lipped and they've cut me out of the loop since they believe that I'm swanning around South West India trying to find my third eye.'

'Could you have told them the truth?'

Nate stared at him long and hard.

Luca nodded, understanding without the Englishman having to explain. He knew this world too. 'They would forgive ludicrous frivolity, but not a medical complication that could see you drop dead at any minute, putting stocks and shares at risk.'

Nate nodded as if satisfied that Luca had answered his own question correctly.

'My sister and I grew up in a nest of vipers, Calvino. It may not seem like it, but she's all alone out there and I can't be there to protect her from this.'

Luca could feel himself swayed by the sibling loyalty and reached into his pocket to start recording the conversation on his phone. 'Are there any specific threats we need to know about?'

'Simon Harcourt, for sure. He's our cousin. I've never been able to pin anything on him, but he's clever enough not to get his own hands dirty. And then there's the usual hangers-on, people after her money.'

'That happen a lot?' Luca asked, taking another look at the, quite frankly, beautiful woman in the pictures.

'There was an ex. I dealt with it.'

'Name?'

'In the file. But I dealt with it.'

'Sure you did,' Luca said, knowing it would get a rise out of the man who had a no-nonsense manner and a quick, dry wit he was beginning to like.

'I'd have thought you'd have more sense than to alienate someone who's about to do you a favour.'

'You're not doing me a favour, you're making me an offer,' Luca pushed back, a smile curving the edge of his mouth. 'I'll put a team together. We can be in play in—'

'You will handle this personally.'

'That's not going to happen.'

While his company was renowned for their careful handling of high profile, very public contracts, he personally didn't. Ever.

'It is. Because if you do this—if you, just you, handle this personally, as a *favour* to me—you will have the sole security contract for Harcourts. That's not just store presence, that's internal, industrial, cyber—and all of it international. You'll have the biggest first step into the English markets by any company ever. You'll be set for life.'

Nate Harcourt was offering him everything he

needed to take Pegaso to the highest heights he could imagine. Luca looked at the black and white photo of a woman exiting the world-famous front doors of Harcourts, bag perched in the crook of a bent arm and large oversized sunglasses covering half of her face. How hard could it be?

'When do I start?'

'Christmas is only a few days away. Am I taking you away from your family?'

'No,' Luca replied without even a thought of the day he'd planned to spend in the office after visiting Alma and Pietro on Christmas Eve, as he did each year.

'A girlfriend?'

'You asking me out, Harcourt?'

'And if I was?'

Luca let out a laugh. The English billionaire was a renowned womaniser. 'Very kind of you to ask, but you're not my type.'

'No. I didn't think so. And as long as my sister isn't either, then we're good.'

CHAPTER ONE

SWEAT DRIPPED DOWN her back and breath poured from her lungs and still Hope Harcourt pushed on. She flicked a gaze to the monitor, four point five kilometres, twenty-three minutes... So close. Her feet pounded against the treadmill in a rhythm that felt primal. She needed this. Needed the moment that effort became effortless, where her body felt fluid with the movements, and her mind felt calm. It didn't last for long and she didn't always get there, but when she did it was...perfect.

The monitor ticked five kilometres at twenty-five minutes and Hope hit the cooldown button. As her pace slowed to match the treadmill, she grabbed the towel she'd hung from the bar and wiped her face, her breathing coming back to normal just in time for the morning call from her assistant. She caught the time on the screen before answering. Six thirty a.m. on the dot.

Elise's chirpy voice came through the wireless headphones as the treadmill slowed even more.

'And how are we this morning?' Elise asked.

'We are wonderful,' Hope replied, hitting the stop button on the treadmill and grabbing her bag. She'd been in the apartment for three years and not once seen anyone else using the building's private gym. She left the blessed air-conditioning and made her way to the lift that would take her up to her sixteenth-floor apartment.

'Was there anything in my inbox from Kinara this morning?' Hope asked. It had taken several years to develop a work strategy that suited her, but now that she had, everything ran much more smoothly for it. She didn't check emails until she got into work, but her assistant would give her a brief rundown before she got ready that day. She got top line info on what to expect, without the drama—*that* could wait until after she'd had coffee. But it helped to know what to dress for.

She'd learned that the hard way. Over the years, the press had made it a sport to catch her at her worst. Whether it was the sixteenth birthday party where she'd been photographed wearing an unflattering and inappropriately short dress, or the frumpy suit she'd worn to her graduation, she'd been shamed one way or another. By the time she'd come to Harcourts, she'd developed an iron-clad sense of fashion that had helped her in her role as Marketing Director just as much as her degree and master's.

As Hope got into the lift she wondered why, of all the articles and hit pieces over the years, it was her sixteenth birthday that always stung that little bit more. Perhaps it was because the photos could only have come from the people around her—her friends.

'Kinara wants to meet. They're doing a shoot on Friday morning but it's the only time they can make it.'

Hope mentally scanned her diary. 'We can do that, right?'

'Yes.'

'Brilliant. Put it in the diary.'

'Doing it now.'

Hope and Harcourts' buyer, Steven, had been trying to court Kinara ever since the deal Nate had tried to make with Casas Fashion had fallen through. And, just like that, her stomach roiled beneath the memory of the day that Nate had collapsed. She had been the one to call the private ambulance, had waited with him as he lay on the floor, his eyes unfocused, the quick, sharp mind that Hope knew almost as well as her own hazed and confused.

He was being treated by the best and, thankfully, on the road to recovery. But, outside of the medical facility, only two people knew about what had happened to her twin brother: her and their grandfather. A secret necessitated by the desperation of businessmen who would willingly step over her brother's sick body to get one rung higher on the Harcourts' ladder. Nate had people in place in his other businesses, but Harcourts was different. And in his absence she'd been fighting off those who would love nothing more than to usurp his position at Harcourts in order to further their own agenda and bank balance.

It was a strange thing to love where you worked but loathe a lot of the people who worked there. She shook her head at the way so many of the shareholders were out of touch with the customers and their needs, uncaring of anything but what ended up in their bank balance. It infuriated her that they couldn't see that by taking the time now, by making smart decisions now they would secure the future of Harcourts for so much longer. But what would they care for that when they wouldn't be around to see it?

'Is there anything else?' Hope asked as the lift let her off at her floor. She took a left and placed her thumb on the keypad beside her door.

The momentary pause from Elise was enough to stir a sense of unease.

'Don't check the socials.'

For a moment Hope's head dropped against the wooden door, safe in the knowledge that she was alone, unseen. A momentary weakness she indulged in before clenching her jaw and pulling herself up. 'What is it this time?'

'Nothing that can't wait.'

'Elise.'

'It's Martin.'

Hope yanked open her door and slammed it behind her, letting loose a string of curses that would make a sailor proud. It didn't matter that Elise had heard. There was very little she kept from the assistant who had been with her for nearly ten years now. Elise had been there when Martin de Savoir had burst into her life with charm and seduction and Elise had also been there when he'd left it, bitterly and loudly, crying 'poor me' to any journalist that would listen.

What Elise didn't know, what no one knew, was the conversation she'd overheard between Martin and her brother. Her stomach turned, already sore from the crunches she'd done before the treadmill. The ache that reminded her that the number of people she could trust could be counted on one hand.

'I—'

'You don't want to know.'

Hope stared out of the window of her apartment. On any day, come rain or shine, the view was spectacular. But she didn't see the impressive outline of The Shard across the Thames, she didn't see the historic Tower of London, or the iconic Tower Bridge stretching from north to south across the river. In her mind she heard Martin's laugh, bitter and nasty, in a way that—at the time—she could barely recognise.

'I have all the proof I need, Martin. I know you're only after her inheritance.'

'God, it's about all she's good for, Harcourt. Everyone knows that.'

'Is there anything else?' Hope asked, breathing through the pain of that devastating moment from the past.

'No.'

'Okay, I'll see you in forty minutes.'

'Don't check the socials.'

Hope hung up the phone and tossed it on the bed. She peeled off her sweaty exercise clothes and stood beneath the powerful jets of water, scalding her skin pink for longer than she usually allowed herself.

Unable and unwilling to spend the day hiding in her shower, as tempting as it might be, she got out, dried herself off and chose her clothes carefully. It was tempting to check Twitter and Instagram, but she genuinely wanted to dress today as if she neither cared nor knew what her ex-fiancé had done this time. She wanted to dress for herself. So she chose a cashmere skirt in camel that hit her mid-calf and nipped her in at the waist, a white silk shirt with a neck bow, and would pair it with buttery soft tan leather calf-high boots and a long cashmere duster coat.

She spent a little more time on her make-up today, knowing that, of all her armour, this was the most important. It took twice as much time to make it look as if she wasn't wearing any, but she'd been doing this for so long it was second nature. She checked herself in the mirror before leaving the apartment—to make sure that she looked as she'd intended, she told herself. Not because she was worried about whatever new wave of press interest would be stirred up by Martin's latest escapade.

But as Hope rode the lift down to the reception of her apartment block, the thing picking at her pulse wasn't anger about what Martin might have got up to this time, but anticipation. Anticipation about a certain tall, broad-shouldered individual who had stepped in to cover when her usual driver, James, had left to attend a family emergency. The naïve kind of anticipation that reminded her of silly schoolgirl crushes which, Hope decided as the lift doors opened, she was far too old for.

But when she saw him waiting for her, through the glass entrance doors of her apartment building, her pulse still reared and bucked like a skittish horse. Hope ducked her head, sliding on her sunglasses to protect her eyes from the early morning's wintry sun and *not* to covertly check him out. But she couldn't help it. She could only hope that he wouldn't notice the blush she felt across her cheeks as she took him in.

Dressed in a black suit, the breadth of his chest caused the lapels to pull open enough to hint at the power beneath but not make it look as if the suit was too small. A white shirt and black tie that disappeared beneath a suit jacket buttoned at lean hips. It should have screamed uniform not boardroom, but there was something about the man that made him look *more*. Her gaze ran upwards, and she decided that it was his face.

His jawline was as sharp as his collar and, clean-shaven, the morning sun glanced off angles that would make a supermodel weep. Dark waves were swept back neatly, shorter at the sides and longer on top, and not a single hair was out of place. Neat. Compact. Efficient. The large dark glasses hid his eyes, making him look inscrutable. Dispassionate even.

And *that* was what frustrated her. Luc's utterly professional behaviour only made her wildly inappropriate reaction to him more obvious, she thought, as she emerged from the apartment complex.

* * *

Luca took a moment to brace himself against his body's unwanted and most definitely wayward reaction to Hope Harcourt. It infuriated him that she seemed to have more control over his body than he did. And it was untenable to have such a reaction to his client. Or, technically, the sister of his client. Either way, she was under his protection, whether she knew it or not, and that put her beyond his reach. Luca had argued against keeping Hope in the dark about his identity, but Nate had been resolute and the carrot he was dangling was big enough to sway him.

Following their meeting, Luca had spent Christmas and New Year planning how the detail would work for Hope Harcourt. Her usual driver had been easily paid off, especially with Nate Harcourt's backing, and Luca's assistant had found him an apartment with easy and immediate access to Hope, but not so close as to risk an accidental run-in. Nate had been able to ease the wheels with IT, allowing him access to Hope's professional emails, and Luca knew, if he deemed it necessary, he could gain access to her private ones, but he was unwilling to breach her privacy at this point.

He had arrived in a snow-covered England six days ago and had immediately thrown himself into the work that would finally see him break into the English-speaking territories. That one thought had driven him like the devil ever since Nate had made the offer back in Switzerland.

For years he'd been trying to break into the market

that would finally make him a global success. From the very beginning he'd had that goal and he'd stuck to it. But, no matter how many satisfied customers or glowing references, or how many multinational clients Pegaso had, it wasn't enough for the UK and US markets. They wanted *old* money and familiar faces, if not accents. And the rejection had stung. But with Nate's offer he would finally crack open the lock that had been on the last territories Luca needed.

Hope emerged from the revolving glass door, cutting into his thoughts, and slipped into the back car seat without sparing him so much as a glance. Luca understood how many could think her cold—especially if they indulged in the rags that called themselves newspapers—but if you looked closely enough, she looked... He rolled his tongue across the roof of his mouth.

Rich. Warm. Luxurious.

The camel colours she wore suited her complexion. Expensive in a way that was so rich it was priceless. There was a subtle golden sheen to her skin that only reinforced the fanciful notion, making him want to run his thumb over her cheek to see the flush of colour bloom beneath it. Her nose was small and slightly upturned, but it suited her. Although hidden, he knew her eyes were a deep brown that should have looked slightly out of place with the blonde of her hair, but didn't. Her jawline led to an angular chin, just perfect for holding between a thumb and forefinger. Perfect to angle to...

Basta! Enough!

He was here to protect her, not lust after her. And that was most definitely what was coursing powerfully through his veins. Hope settled into the back seat as he closed the door, cutting off the gentle enticement of her perfume. Today's scent was different from yesterday's, he noticed. Today's had something with bite.

He got into the driver's seat and turned the key in the ignition, ruthlessly regaining control of his senses. Before starting work as the replacement driver, he'd checked over the car with a fine-tooth comb and was satisfied that not only was it in excellent condition, it contained no tracking or covert listening devices. It seemed unlikely, but Luca was nothing if not thorough. And although the car remained in his apartment's parking space overnight, he still checked it every single morning.

Pulling out into the traffic on Upper Thames Street, he decided on his route to Harcourts' flagship department store in Mayfair. In the rear-view mirror he watched Hope gazing out of the window at the morning London scene. He found it strange that Hope never reached for her phone on her morning commute. There was something almost serene about the image.

A motorbike zipped past him and Luca refocused on the road until his personal mobile vibrated against his chest. The single burst of vibration meant the message from his team wasn't urgent, and he could only conclude that they hadn't yet found proof linking the Harcourt twins' cousin, Simon, to the journalist re-

sponsible for a shocking seventy-eight percent of the
negative press against Hope. Lucas was sure it was
there though.

Even the tech analyst he'd put on the search had
been angered and shocked by the sheer volume of
hate and vitriol directed at a woman just going about
her business. The same analyst had been tasked with
looking deeper into Hope's history to check areas
of vulnerability in case there was something they
needed to know.

As an oncoming car took a right turn across the
lane, the headlights swept across his eyeline and he
saw flashbulbs, thousands of them, the calls and yells
of the crowd between him and his mother…

'Give us a smile, Anna! Come on!'

'Over here, Anna!'

*'Is it true that you're involved with your co-star,
Anna?'*

'When are you going to settle down, Anna?'

Without pause, Luca moved the car forward, inch-
ing towards their turn-off, despite the direction of
his thoughts. Despite the memory of how his eter-
nally glamorous mother had thrown her head back
and laughed the sexy, throaty laugh she was known
for and replied to the baying crowd, 'Never, darlings.
I'll *never* settle down!'

And she hadn't. Italy's most famous actress had
never married, never had a relationship lasting more
than the promotion of her latest film, and had never—
not once—acknowledged the fact that at sixteen she'd

had a child out of wedlock, who had been raised by two members of her family in secret.

Disconcerted to find himself surprised as they pulled up to the majestic front doors of Harcourts in Mayfair, Luca mentally slapped himself. It was unacceptable to have been so distracted with a client. Frustration made his actions sharp as he exited the town car and held Hope's door open for her. Getting out of the car, her skirt rose barely enough to show an inch of creamy skin between the hemline and her boots, and he looked steadfastly ahead. He saw the briefest frown above her sunglasses, as if she'd noticed the staccato edge to his actions.

She paused. 'Elise will let you know when I'm done for the day. All meetings are internal so I won't be needing you until then.'

'I'll wait,' he said simply.

'It won't be necessary,' she replied, that little frown still in place above her sunglasses.

'I'll be here.'

She looked at him for a moment more, before disappearing beneath the world-famous gold and purple awning into the building. He had frustrated her and, while that hadn't been his intention, he hadn't missed the moment where fire had ignited in the air between them. Two competitors wrestling for control, tension and force of will coming up against each other.

And he'd wanted it, he realised, cursing himself. Wanted to test the strength of it.

His phone vibrated against his chest again and he turned back to the car to drive it round to the underground car park, where he could check out what his people had found. It was time to stop messing around and get his head on straight.

Hope shook off the strange tension that still zinged in her blood from her interaction with Luc and entered her office, walking straight to the large window that looked out onto a snow-covered Hyde Park.

There was something magical about this time of year, especially for a department store like Harcourts, where people would come from all over the world to look at their festive display windows and the beautiful, bright Christmas decorations. There was an almost constant hum of excitement and holiday happiness from the staff and customers alike, but even that wasn't as glorious as London in the snow.

Her office was in what the staff called 'the old wing', directly above the Mayfair store. The traditional character of the original building's features remained strong, unlike the 'new wing' to the back of the large sprawling building, where the offices were all sleek chrome, glass and granite and full of the ego contests that spun back and forth between her brother and cousin.

Hers was larger than the smaller modern offices, but that wasn't its appeal. This office had once belonged to her father. It was where she had visited him as a child and it was where she remembered him best. It was her connection to her parents, especially when the past grew a little less clear each and every day she grew older. *That* was why she loved it.

It was later that day when she turned back to her computer, casting one last look at the email that would green-light a brand-new marketing campaign in the US. She'd travel out there later in the year, once it was underway, but she was excited by it. It was sexy and contemporary—things she wanted for Harcourts, rather than the dusty and predominantly old campaigns run in the past.

She'd had a good day so far. She'd nudged Daniel, the acting Financial Director covering for her brother, back on track after a showdown with Simon had knocked his confidence. She'd try to keep that from Nate if she could. The last thing her brother needed was to be worrying about Harcourts.

Elise stuck her head in the doorway, a light frown across her brow. 'Just a heads-up. I've heard that the Chairman is attending the shareholders' meeting this afternoon.'

'Really?' Hope asked. Her grandfather usually spent the period between Christmas and the staff party at home in Tunbridge Wells. Home being a sprawling family estate about as old as the Harcourts building. Frowning herself, she scanned the agenda for the meeting taking place in fifteen minutes' time. 'There's nothing here that would warrant his attention,' she noted, looking back at Elise.

Elise shrugged, seemingly just as confused.

'Anything else?'

'No,' Hope replied absently.

'Are you sure?' Elise asked.

'Yes,' Hope hedged, half curious about the wicked gleam in Elise's eye.

'Really? You don't want to know what I've heard about TD and H?'

'Elise!'

'What? He *is* tall, dark and handsome.'

'*He* has a name.'

'And it's *Luc*,' Elise said, drawing out the sound of his name and swooning dramatically against the door frame.

Hope couldn't help but laugh.

'And I've heard that—'

'Nope! Don't want to know,' Hope insisted.

'Yes, you do,' Elise teased.

'I really don't.'

'It's just that I've heard he has a really big—'

Elise's sentence was cut off by the sheaf of paper that had been an agenda and was now a missile striking its target. Elise's scream startled a passing member of staff and dissolved in to giggles.

'Bike,' Elise muttered quietly picking up the agenda from the floor. 'His motorbike. I've heard it's really big.'

'Out!' Hope demanded, trying to smother her own laughter as she gathered her things for the meeting because the only frustrating thing about this office was that it was a ten-minute walk from where most of the meetings were held. But it gave her a chance to enjoy the feeling of a day well spent. Too many things had been up in the air recently, but today…it was shaping up to be a *good* one.

Thirty minutes later, the sound around Hope was deafening. Shareholders rose from their seats, some were shouting and jeering while others were clapping. She caught her grandfather's purposely blank gaze before she turned to glare at her cousin. Simon was smiling and clapping the CEO, who had just thrown the room into chaos by announcing that he was stepping down, without warning or thought to the impact on Harcourts.

No! Hope's head spun. It wasn't supposed to be like this. For years, Nate had been primed to take over from Johnson. He'd done the required schmoozing and courting of the shareholders; he'd put in the time and effort. From the looks being shared between Simon and Johnson, the now outgoing CEO, Hope clenched her jaw and decided it was nothing short of a coup. And they had waited until Nate was out of the picture to make their move.

Her grandfather slammed his hand down on the table three times, silencing the baying crowd. 'Clearly this news is unexpected, but we thank the outgoing CEO for his work and dedication over the years as he has safeguarded Harcourts' clear dominance in the luxury goods market.'

Hope wondered how much that had hurt to say. Johnson had been nothing but a stick-in-the-mud, holding Harcourts back by penny-pinching and the least progressive business direction she had ever seen.

'Leonard Johnson has steered our ship with singular focus and the utmost dedication and as Chairman it is my duty to ensure that the handover to the incoming CEO is smooth, efficient and quick. Nominations for the incoming CEO will take place in two days' time. The vote for CEO will happen in two weeks' time. That concludes the meeting.'

Hope bit back a curse. There was no way that Nate would be able to get here in that time. She looked to Simon again, who finally deigned to turn a smug, satisfied gaze in her direction. Her pulse raced from outrage and indignation, even as she became aware of the weight of several pairs of eyes turning on her.

Her grandfather stood, and so did everyone else in the room, a courtesy and a tradition upheld from an earlier time until the Chairman of Harcourts left the room, and instead of screaming and shouting her anger she smiled and nodded to the few people who had encouraging words on their lips but pity in their eyes.

CHAPTER TWO

Luca resisted getting out of the car. If it wasn't for the thirty or so members of the esteemed British press, he'd have gone in there and given Hope Harcourt both barrels. He messaged her again.

The garage is safer. I can bring the car there in two minutes.

Her reply was instantaneous.

No.

He wanted to growl. This was part of the trouble with having a client who didn't know they were a client. They didn't listen to him when he made genuine decisions about their safety. He cursed Nathanial to hell and back, before remembering that he'd probably already been there.

The press had started to gather before he'd arrived and in the last five minutes even more had appeared. Luca had been about to call the analyst assessing the

Harcourts case, when Nate had called to warn him that the current CEO was stepping down in order to ensure that Simon was the only viable option to take his place. The background info was welcome, but the warning about the resulting press attention came too late. Clearly someone—most likely Simon Harcourt—had tipped them off. Luca was beginning to seriously dislike the man and he'd never even met him.

Luca's mobile was in his hand, his finger hovering over another message to Hope, when he saw her emerge into the famous foyer of Harcourts department store. She was walking at quite a pace and he readied himself to exit the car to have her door open for her, when a tall man sidled up beside her and stopped her.

Simon Harcourt.

Luca narrowed his gaze. Through the strobe lighting of camera flashes, he could just make out the way Simon leaned into her space. Instinct warred against staying in the car and simply observing the interaction. He cursed Nate again, whether he'd been to hell or not, for the limits that he'd put on Luca's ability to do his job. If he'd been beside Hope instead of stuck out here, the cousin wouldn't have got within two feet of her.

Luca assessed the situation quickly. From outward appearances, it was two colleagues—cousins—simply having a quick chat on the way out. But he could read the lines her body was making. Sharp and tense, she was trying very hard to suppress her anger. He'd done it on purpose, Luca realised, cornering her in front of the press. He fired off a message to the case analyst, demanding all info on Simon Harcourt to be sent to him immediately.

The moment Hope moved, he moved.

He was out of the car and, even though he'd expected it, he was still slammed by the wall of sound that had been muffled in the car's interior. Journalists jostled and shouted, trying to get a soundbite on the internal fighting that was about to take over one of the world's most recognisable companies.

'Hope, what would your brother be saying if he was here?'

'Will Nate come back from his travels for this?'

'Hope, who do you think the next CEO will be?'

She ignored them all, Simon having hung back to watch her walk into the braying madness from inside the department store. Sunglasses hid her gaze, as they did his, but despite that, he knew she was looking right at him, locked onto him as if he were her lifeline.

He closed the door behind her after she'd slid smoothly into the back of the car and resisted the urge to violently remove the paparazzo who tried to get a photo as Luca opened the door to get into the driver's seat. He gently manoeuvred the car through the crowd and onto the road, leaving the chaos behind them. He counted down from ten and was surprised to get as far as three before she spoke.

'Don't question my decisions again,' she said, her voice clipped.

Understanding that she was referring to his request to pick her up in the garage, he replied with a careful, 'No, ma'am.'

'Do you know the address in Tunbridge Wells?'

'Yes, ma'am,' he confirmed, having made a point of knowing all the likely locations she might need.

'We're going there now.'

'Yes, ma'am,' he said, making a left-hand turn towards the river.

A few minutes of silence passed between them before she spoke again.

'It would have looked as if I was hiding.'

'Yes, ma'am,' he agreed. But it would have been safer.

Darkness fell as they travelled further and further away from the mess of the shareholders' meeting, which was a metaphor for something, Hope was pretty sure. But out here, as they turned off the M25 and onto the A2, on the way to her grandfather's estate, it felt almost as if it were just her and Luc alone in the world.

Luc.

She'd felt his frustration that afternoon. As if he'd wanted to protect her somehow. The thought was laughable if she were being unkind to herself, and fanciful if she were being charitable. Ridiculous was what it was, whichever way she looked at it. Her thoughts changing tack, she reached for her phone and hit the dial button.

Nate answered on the second ring, as if he'd been waiting for her call.

'I didn't know,' he said immediately. 'I thought something was going on, but I didn't know what.'

'And you didn't think to warn me?' she demanded, some of her feelings bleeding out into her tone.

'I didn't want to worry you,' he replied.

She bit back a harsh response and swallowed around the hurt reminding her that her brother didn't think she was strong enough to handle things like this. Just like he hadn't thought she was strong enough to handle the truth about Martin.

'What are we going to do?' she asked. 'The nomination for CEO is on Friday, the vote is in two weeks.'

Nate's response was a curse. She understood his frustration. They both wanted great things for Harcourts, things they'd imagined that he would be able to do as CEO.

'I'm on my way to see Grandfather.'

Silence met her statement. She knew his relationship with their grandfather was strained in a way that hers wasn't, but she'd never understood why.

'There's…nothing I can do from here,' Nate admitted, sounding defeated.

'You can get better, Nate. That's all I want,' she insisted truthfully.

He ended the call without a reply and the silence rang loudly in her head. She knew her twin brother as well as she knew herself. And she knew how hard he was finding his body's slow recovery from the life-threatening aneurism that had nearly stolen his life. And renewed anger that Simon and Johnson had taken advantage of that weakness fired her blood.

As the car arrived at the family estate, she didn't see the grand sweeping drive, the ancient stone fountain in the centre, three majestic horses lit from beneath. She didn't even give Luc directions as to where to wait or park. Her focus was solely on getting to her grandfather, hoping he could tell her what was going on.

Her heels crunched on gravel, then on stone steps, then on parquet flooring and then on the wooden floor, clipping at a pace that kept time with her racing pulse. She ignored the greeting of Mrs Conway, the housekeeper she had known for as long as she'd been alive, and her husband, the butler, who waited outside her grandfather's office as if he'd expected her.

She caught his gaze from the other side of the hallway and he nodded, saying, 'You can go in, ma'am.'

She didn't pause on the threshold, didn't knock, didn't do any of the things she would usually have done when visiting the grandfather who stood on ceremony above all else.

He was standing behind his desk, looking out of the window into the darkness. The fire in the fireplace flickered and the lighting was subtle and soft.

'Grandfather.'

'You made good time from London,' he observed without turning around.

'Why didn't you tell me?' Hope asked, finally giving voice to the question that had run in her head on a loop since the announcement.

'Because I don't do favours for family.'

No. Hope knew that first-hand. Her grandfather believed that the hard way was the only way.

'Simon knew,' she replied.

'If he did, it didn't come from me,' was her grandfather's clipped response.

Hope bit back the breath aching in her chest. 'It wasn't supposed to be this way.'

'Of course it wasn't. It was supposed to be your father.'

The slap of his words was a shock and she inhaled through the pain. But it was a pain she saw reflected in his eyes as he turned to face her.

'I don't play favourites, Hope. I can't. Because *they* won't.'

She clenched her teeth against the harsh love he'd always shown her, Nate and presumably even Simon. She knew he was talking about the shareholders. The board. She knew he was talking about more than a job or a role—their inheritance.

'What kind of guardian would I have been if I'd mollycoddled you and given you special treatment?'

'Special?' she huffed out scornfully. 'Any kind of treatment would have been preferable to—'

'Do you want it?' her grandfather demanded, cutting off her unexpected emotional response.

'What?'

'The CEO position.'

'It was *supposed* to be Nate.'

'Well, that's not going to happen now, is it? You can't sit on the fence any more, Hope. If you want it,

do something about it. If not? Make peace with the
fact that Simon is going to get it.'

Luca rubbed his hands together and breathed out a
cloudy stream of breath. He prowled back and forth
beside the car in the way he'd not been able to do earlier, outside Harcourts. He was used to being much
more active than this, and not being able to work off
the excess energy wasn't helping his mood.

Yeah, right. You keep telling yourself that.

'You can come in, you know?'

Luca looked up at the older man, sticking his head
out of the back door.

'That's okay, but thank you.'

'You'll freeze your testicles off in this weather.
Get in here or my wife will have mine over coals.'

Luca bit back a laugh at the rough talk from the
old man who reminded him somehow of Pietro. He
recognised the man as the butler from Hope's file.
Mr Conwary had been with the family for his entire
working life. There were only two reasons a man did
that. Loyalty or greed. There was nothing about a man
who proudly admitted that his wife would roast his
testicles over hot coals that suggested greed.

He looked back at the car, worried that he wouldn't
be there for Hope when she'd finished with her grandfather.

'She'd be more unhappy that you'd waited outside
in the cold than having to look for you with us,' the
man said, jerking his head back towards the house.

Relenting, Luca nodded his thanks and followed

the old man through the back parts of the house and into a large, very recognisably English, country kitchen. A woman matching the butler's age turned to welcome him. Mrs Conwary. He'd have known it even without the background info. Cheeks pink from cooking something that smelled delicious, she smiled big and hugged hard. Luca was somewhat startled by the easy affection from these two and was hastily trying to fit it into what he knew about Hope and Nate's upbringing.

'Have a seat. Tea? Stew's not ready, but it'll do if you're hungry.'

Luca translated her words from English to Italian and got the gist. 'No, thank you, ma'am.'

She cooed in delight. 'Did you hear that? Me, ma'am? Charmer.'

Luca couldn't help but smile at the couple. This appeared as much their home as their employer's but their easy way around him was something he'd never experienced, not even with Pietro and Alma.

'You've started with Hope?' Mrs Conwary asked.

'Yes,' Luca said, readying himself for who knew what.

'How is she doing?'

'I can't believe that little toerag waited until Nate was…was…' her husband growled, cutting a glance at Luca '…away. What is Hope expected to do?'

Luca wasn't sure what a toerag was, but it didn't sound good. Mrs Conwary was staring at Luca intently, still clearly hoping for an answer.

'She is okay,' he hedged, not about to share his

true thoughts on the subject of Hope, no matter how friendly the couple appeared to be.

Mrs Conwary hummed disapprovingly. 'She's not as tough as she looks.'

'I don't know about that, Mary,' the old man mused. 'She'll have to be if she's to throw her name in the hat.'

Luca kept his expression blank, but he was surprised that the family staff seemed to be as well-informed on the political wranglings at Harcourts as they were.

'I'd like to give that Simon a piece of my mind.'

Mary grabbed her husband's wagging finger and gently pushed it away from Luca's face. One part of him was amused, the other—the one focused on Hope Harcourt—was very much not.

'She used to be such a happy girl. Had a laugh that was like sunshine,' Mary said wistfully, staring at a series of old photo frames placed along a sideboard. 'Sorry, it's the time of year. Brings back the bad.'

The bad? Luca's confusion must have shown on his face.

'Memories. Bad memories. Hope's parents died in a car accident. Terrible thing. Patch of black ice took the car on the way back from a fancy party in London.'

Mr Conwary rubbed circles on his wife's back to soothe her and an odd twist in his conscience caught Luca by surprise. He had known about her parents' death, noted it but not taken in the date. It was around this time of year, he vaguely remembered.

'Mr and Mrs Conwary,' came Hope's voice from behind them all.

She was standing in the doorway, head resting against the frame, with a smile on her face that suggested she might *not* have heard what they had just been discussing.

Mrs Conwary looked aghast for a moment, but covered well and rushed to envelop Hope's thinner frame in her larger one. Mr Conwary shot Luca a glance that said he wasn't fooled either.

Luca got up, but Hope gestured for him to sit back down and he waited while she caught up with two people who just beamed in her presence. And while there was still something watchful about her, braced in a way he couldn't explain, she softened around them in a way that felt more naturally *her* than he'd seen so far.

Hope spent twenty minutes listening to the Conwarys talk about their children and grandchildren. She ate the small bowl of stew that was put there 'just in case' she changed her mind and decided she was hungry. She exchanged their hugs with promises to be back soon on the steps of the back entrance to the house as Luca got the car ready and warm. And all the while he couldn't shake the conviction that she was wearing another mask as she once again slid into the back seat as he held the door open for her without looking at him.

It was about half an hour into the journey. Hope was looking out of the window and said, 'You can ask, you know.'

'Pardon, ma'am?'

'Don't call me ma'am. It makes me feel old,' she admitted, her tone softer than the words sounded. 'Ask. You've been wanting to all evening.'

Luca inhaled, torn, knowing he should ask about her meeting with her grandfather, but needing to hear what her cousin had said to her. Either question could blur professional boundaries, but she had offered him the chance to ask of her own free will.

'What did Simon say to you in the foyer before you left Harcourts this afternoon?'

Hope continued to stare out of her window. It looked as if she might not have heard him. It looked as if she hadn't spoken. But then… 'He apologised that the timing of the vote coincided with the anniversary of my parents' death.'

Luca's hands white-knuckled around the steering wheel.

She could have lied. She probably should have, because the moment that the words came out of her mouth she felt it again. That thrum of awareness, almost a sense of connection. However it had happened, something had built between her and Luc.

'I'm sorry.' The words were gravel thick and forced.

'For Simon?' she scoffed bitterly.

'For your parents.'

Her heart turned, and she resented that. Resented that his words meant so much to her. Hated that just two little words worked to soothe the ache she hid so deep.

Luc knew more about her than James did—her driver of nearly five years. James was cordial, jovial even, but she couldn't imagine Luc being anything other than… She'd been thinking *cold*, or *distant*, but that wasn't quite right. He might be aloof, but beneath was a heat, a driving force that was absent in her normal driver. She'd seen it in the way he'd responded when she'd refused to let him pick her up from the garage earlier that day. She felt it now, shimmering in the air between them as Luc digested what Simon had callously taunted her with. It was anger. For her. An anger she didn't know what to do with, because it stirred her own already twisting emotions from her grandfather's words.

And suddenly she didn't want to go home to an empty apartment, for a few hours' sleep, before her alarm went off and she started the day all over again. Gym, Elise's call at six thirty, fighting whatever the press could throw her way again, the vote. Just the thought of it was stifling.

She cleared her throat. 'Can we take the scenic route back, please?'

'Scenic?' he asked, frowning at the nightscape beyond the car.

Her lips pulled into a small wry smile. So much for subtlety… 'I don't want to go home just yet. Is there a longer route we can take?' she clarified.

'*Sì,*' he replied. 'Yes,' he repeated unnecessarily.

She gazed out at the passing scenery. The roads

were clear at this time of night, the sound of the tyres rolling over concrete soothing in its monotony. She'd never learned to drive—not after what had happened to her parents—and it usually took her a long time to become comfortable enough with a driver, but she'd not had that with Luc. From the very beginning she'd felt...*safe*.

She looked to the rear-view mirror which, from where she sat, showed Luc's brows and eyes and just a section of that patrician nose. With his focus on the roads, she gave herself free rein to look her fill. Now that it wasn't hidden behind the sunglasses he wore during the day, she could lose herself in the silvery gaze. The pools of gunmetal grey were arresting, strangely unique and out of place with his Mediterranean colouring and the heavy brow that hung above his eyes made him seem sterner than he was. She should look away, but she couldn't quite bring herself to. Until she became almost convinced that he knew she was watching him. Heat burned her skin, her breath caught in her chest and her pulse pounded in her throat before she finally wrenched her gaze away.

Personal. That's what her perusal of him made her feel. As if she were taking something back from the man who already knew too much about her.

'How long have you been in England?' Hope asked, attempting to break whatever it was that had thickened the air in the car's interior.

'Not long,' he replied, his monosyllabic answer providing only frustration. Hope needed a distraction; she wanted the mindless conversation to take her thoughts away from the dark. She wanted not to have to think so hard about so much.

'Is it very different? Driving here than in Italy?' she tried again, knowing that the questions were asinine.

'Yes.'

'Whereabouts in Italy are you from?'

'The south,' he replied.

Hope huffed out a little breathy laugh. 'Luc, are you sure you're not a spy?'

Luca forced the curve of a smile to his lips in case she could see it, hoping that it would keep him on the right side of her joke. He flicked his gaze between the road and Hope's reflection in the rear-view mirror. In the past, women had complained that he always held himself back, that refusing to share personal information made him harder to know. But years spent keeping his entire existence a secret had taken its toll.

'I was born in Bari, but raised in Palizzi,' he replied, startled when he realised that he'd given her the truth.

'I've been to Italy many times, but not Palizzi.'

He smiled freely this time. Not many people knew of it. 'It's about as far south as you can get in Italy.'

'What's it like?' she asked.

He knew what she wanted to hear: the tourist spiel. About its beach, the famous old medieval castle that loomed imperiously above the village from its rocky outcrop. But all he could think about was how, as a child, he'd longed to escape the quiet rurality of it all and join his mother in the fantastic adventures he was sure they'd have. He'd travel the world with her as her white knight, protecting her from anyone who would do her harm. That was what he'd told himself in the cold silence of Pietro and Alma's house.

Whenever he could, he'd escaped to run along the shoreline, exploring the azure blue bay that reached out into the Ionian Sea. He'd felt unwanted by them, but bound to the aunt and uncle into whose care he had been entrusted. And in those early years he'd believed it was them keeping him from his mother, rather than the other way round.

Luca felt Hope's retreat in the silence.

'I'm sorry, I shouldn't have—'

'It's beautiful,' he said, interrupting her apology. 'It's quiet, nothing like London,' he said, trying to cling to the role of chauffeur while answering her questions with as much truth as possible. He was good at it usually—after all, he'd learned from his mother, and his mother was the best of the best. But something about Hope Harcourt was throwing him off.

'Above the village is an old castle,' he said, noticing how that had caught Hope's interest in the glance he shared with her through the rear-view mirror. 'Not that kind of castle,' he said around a smile. 'It was reconstructed in the mid seventeen hundreds and looks more like a military garrison than anything else.'

'Sounds…charming,' Hope said wryly, and Luca's lips quirked into a half-smile.

'It had its moments,' he admitted.

'Why London?'

'I had a client who brought me with him when he came to London,' he hedged. 'And when he went back, I decided to stay.'

She flicked her gaze to his in the mirror as if she hadn't quite believed him, but the moment he met her eyes he felt it—the jolt, as if he'd been zapped in the chest. It was like being gripped by fire and soothed by ice at the same time. She held his gaze for a beat too long, and this time it was Hope who looked away, leaning back against her seat and turning her attention back out of the window.

His pulse thudded sluggishly, forcing blood away from his groin and back to the brain he needed to drive. It had been so long since a woman had had such power over him. Yes, he'd been with attractive women over the years—and his last mutually beneficial no-strings relationship had only been six months before. But when he thought about it, he knew that the desire they had shared was nothing compared to the incendiary heat that had absolutely no place being between him and Hope.

An hour later he pulled up outside her apartment block and she exited the car with a 'Goodnight,' and a quiet, 'See you in the morning.'

He waited until the lift doors closed on her, watching him watch her.

He shook his head and pulled the car back out into the night. His own apartment was barely three minutes and two streets away. He guided the car into the underground garage and pulled into the reserved parking space as he thought about what Hope had been through today.

He made his way up to his penthouse apartment and poured himself a drink, all the while unable to shake the feeling of her eyes on him, watching him as he drove, as he waited for her with the car. Having spent a lot of his professional life watching other people, he'd never once realised how intimate it was. Intrusive? Absolutely. But with Hope it was something else.

He took the tumbler of ice and whisky out onto the balcony, the slap of the cold, wintry night air enough to cut through the hazy hangover from her attention.

This. This was what it was about, Luca reminded himself as he looked out across the London skyline. This was what was at stake. Expanding his company, ensuring its global viability. He wanted a piece of it. And the key to making that was keeping his hands off Hope Harcourt.

CHAPTER THREE

Hope woke battling a headache. As the day of the nominations had drawn closer, she had felt sure that Simon had done this on purpose—engineered the nominations to happen on the anniversary of her parents' death. That he had waited for Nate to be away, that he had waited until no one was there to stop him. Tension and anger made her headache worse and no amount of running on the treadmill would help.

She missed Nate so acutely that morning and was torn between wanting to reach out to him and not wanting to bother him. He needed rest, he needed to get better, and he wouldn't do that if he thought for one minute she needed him. He'd always tried to protect her. Too much sometimes. But he at least understood her grief. She could usually share that with him, but not today.

Hope shook her head at herself. There was too much in her head, she needed to compartmentalise. She put thoughts of her parents gently aside until she returned home that evening. Right now, she needed to think of today—her meeting with Kinara and the nominations.

She pulled the oversized, soft as silk, black scarf from the hanger and looped it around her neck, over the cream cashmere rollneck long-sleeve top she wore tucked into black houndstooth wool wide-legged trousers. She grabbed her bag, slipped into her coat, left her apartment and waited for the lift to arrive, trying not to count the ways that Harcourts had already been damaged by Simon's penny-pinching and the CEO's laziness. Because Harcourts wasn't just a job to her. It was a legacy. Her parents' legacy. She wondered who would put themselves forward, but all she could see was her cousin. And if Simon became CEO…

The lift doors slid open and whisked her down to the ground floor.

You can't sit on the fence any more, Hope. If you want it, do something about it.

Her pulse tripped when she spied Luc waiting for her outside her apartment. If she'd thought that things might have changed between them after the drive back from Tunbridge Wells, she'd been wrong. Whatever intimacy she had imagined was absent the next time she'd seen him. It was as if it hadn't happened. Which would have been fine, had it not left a gaping hole in its place—as if something between them was missing and she couldn't quite say whether that was a good thing or a bad thing.

She found herself distracted by his aftershave, especially when he held the door open for her. It teased her senses, adding weight to the thump of her heart and a betraying flush to her cheeks. A part of her wanted to tell him to change it and the other part wanted to get closer, to stand chest to chest with him, to angle her head so that it fitted in the crook of his neck, so that she could get as close as possible to where it would be strongest, to where the scent was heated by his body, his skin, and where she could just *inhale*.

As Luc guided the car north, away from central London, towards Hackney, she ordered herself to get her head in the game. In less than twenty minutes she would meet with Kinara, the fashion designer she'd been hoping would help her bring Harcourts back into the twenty-first century.

They were a British designer, young but fresh and exciting and with no naiveté about the world they were working in. Born and working in Hackney, there was both a street element to their designs as well as a business casual style that spoke to Hope. It was the direction she desperately wished Harcourts would move towards. Intelligent, contemporary, broad appealing and sexy.

So Hope would get through the meeting with Kinara and go to the shareholders' meeting where the nominations would take place. Once she saw who was running against Simon, she'd be able to make a decision about what to do next. She would get through the entire day and she would get home and then she would let the walls come down around the pain of spending the anniversary of her parents' death alone.

Luca turned the car down a narrow street that looked barely fit for pedestrian use, disliking the menacingly industrial feel of the north London area. He hadn't been familiar with Hackney at all, and while the main road was urban but bright and clean, this... not so much.

He flicked a gaze to Hope, who was talking to Elise on the phone about the timing of the shareholders' meeting. She'd been doing her best to ignore him since he'd withdrawn behind a wall of professional civility following the visit to her grandfather's.

He glared at the display on his own phone as if it would make Nate Harcourt call him back. He'd hoped that he might have some information on what had passed between Hope and her grandfather, but Nate had remained unreachable and Luca had been forced to remind himself that it was hardly the man's fault that he was in a Swiss hospital.

The narrow lane finally opened out onto a large square surrounded on all sides by red brick buildings several storeys high, giving the strange impression of a modern-day amphitheatre. One that was, apparently, being put to good use.

Three models were posed around an old metal bin with real flames curling into the sky. A man leaned forward, hunched over his camera, clicking away while shouting directions at both the models and the staff. Another group of people were crowded around a laptop on a small table set up off to the left.

Luca shrugged off the thought that what he was seeing just made him feel old. He pulled up off to the far right, where a kid dressed in jeans hanging too low and an off-the-shoulder T-shirt was pointing.

He exited the car and went to Hope's door, holding it open for her as she got out and trying to ignore all the natural danger points of what was essentially the spatial equivalent of a shooting gallery.

Hope barely paused long enough to tell him to 'Wait here,' before walking away, and he told himself that her sharpness was the least he deserved, as his eyes tracked her to a table where three people stood staring at a monitor and speaking quietly.

One of the teens, a young woman with blue eyes and brown lazily curling hair that fell halfway down her back, was now the sole focus of the photographer.

'Look over your shoulder, Tina,' called the man with the camera, and Luca's pulse jumped.

The woman didn't even remotely look like his mother. But between the posing, the photographer, the press, it was all hitting a little too close to home.

It had been nearly fourteen months since he'd last seen Anna. It had been another cloak-and-dagger meeting in a hotel in some city that happened to be a midpoint of nowhere for them both. And it had been the time he'd finally realised what he most disliked about these less than yearly meetings.

'Sit down and tell me all about how you're doing,' she'd said, patting a space on the chair opposite her.

As if he were still the same child she'd said exactly the same thing to when he was nine. As if twenty years hadn't passed. Always focused on him and never sharing about herself.

That last time it had hit him more forcefully than

ever before, because it was exactly what his last lover had accused him of as she'd left.

'You don't share yourself, Luca. You give me everything I could possibly need, apart from yourself.'

He'd not even been consciously doing it. And it made him wonder whether his mother realised she did it too, that she kept their relationship on those terms, *her* terms, or whether it had just become habit. And as difficult as it had been growing up with only one foot in her life and the other in Palizzi with Alma and Pietro, he'd wondered what it must have been like for her. To see her child grow up over a handful of days across a handful of years, rather than day in, day out. To see how he had become an adult in less than a month's worth of time, while she had miraculously stayed the same.

'Now, look away?' the photographer called and Luca wondered about these people's families. Did they have them? Were they waiting at home? What would these people choose to sacrifice for fame and money?

He became aware of someone's eyes on him and searched through the crowd of people to see who it was. He managed not to react to the amusing and utterly obvious way a young male model was ogling him. If he'd been off-duty he would have smiled graciously at the guy while discreetly refusing any advance—just in the same way he would have done with the female model next to him, also devouring him with her gaze.

But he wasn't. He was working and he returned his

focus returned to Hope, who was talking to a person he presumed was Kinara, and he forgot about the two models laughing and giggling over the looks that were one of only two things he could thank his mother for.

'That man is *fine*,' Kinara observed.

Hope raised an eyebrow as if unaware that they were speaking about Luc.

'Oh, girl, don't play coy with me. Every single person here with a pulse has checked him out. He could be in front of that damn camera. In fact, if he wants to go and put on some of my—'

'Hands off,' Hope interrupted.

Kinara laughed, a rich, joyous tease of a laugh. 'All that was missing from the end of your sentence was *my man*.'

Hope shook her head. 'He works for me.'

'And that stopped who, exactly?'

'Precisely. How am I supposed to be better than all the men that dipped their fountain pen in the company ink if I just do as they do?'

The tease left Kinara's assessing gaze. 'Fair. But seriously, though.'

Hope couldn't help but smile, just about resisting the urge to look over her shoulder to where a significant amount of attention was gathering on her Italian chauffeur. 'Seriously though' was ringing in her head as she tried to get them back on track.

She caught the eye of Anita, a Harcourts marketing assistant, and sent her a wave. Anita would be gathering behind-the-scenes photos and interviews to put across their socials just before the launch. Hope, Kinara and Anita had worked hard on the marketing campaign that would start four months before on-sale, and go hard two months in. There were levels to it, digital, in-person, celebrity endorsement, TV advertising, billboards and even client-generated content after sale, each part purposely curated to ensure that Kinara's collection sold as forecast. It all stretched out before them in lines that Hope could see and would pull together to make one hell of a campaign.

'I want to bring you in to meet with the senior staff.'

Kinara squinted. 'Am I ready for that?' they asked a little nervously.

'Absolutely,' Hope replied, knowing that it was right she had come here today. 'This is your first shoot for your first collection for us and I couldn't be happier or prouder with what you're doing.'

Kinara, who had always been tactile and utterly themselves, swept Hope up in a hug. The sudden contact surprised her, her already precarious emotions teetering on the brink. Hope hugged Kinara back with as much enthusiasm as she was given and eventually they started laughing at themselves.

Pulling back to level Kinara with a gaze, 'I love this collection,' Hope said sincerely. 'And I know with absolute certainty that I am the lucky one who got you before all the others come calling and want you in their stores.'

Kinara waved off Hope's words before pulling her over to the monitor, where they explained the styles and coordinated sets that had been put together for the collection. Hope stayed at the shoot for as long as her schedule would allow, letting herself enjoy Kinara's fierce concentration and determined view of what they wanted. It was a part of her job she really enjoyed, helping to choose new stockists. And, although as Marketing Director it wasn't common, she'd worked hard with the Harcourts buyer to make this happen. Because she believed in it.

She quietly started saying her goodbyes so as not to disrupt the notoriously pedantic photographer.

'Listen, you know that Gabriella Casas has been trying to reach your brother?' Kinara asked.

Hope frowned. The interim Financial Director had mentioned Ms Casas trying to reach Nate too, but Hope shook it off. It would wait until Nate was better, even if nothing else could.

She shrugged off Kinara's question and looked back to where Luc was still standing by the car. No one could deny that he was striking, the deep blue suit and crisp white shirt mere window-dressing for the main attraction that was *him*. She heard the giggles of the models, clearly checking him out, but instead of preening under the attention, Hope was half convinced that, beneath his dark glasses, his focus was—as it always seemed—on her. Embarrassed by the sudden thump of her heart, sluggish and heavy at the thought, she made her way slowly towards him, suddenly conscious of everything between them. The sound of her breath, the slight tightening across his shoulders, the clench low in her belly, the flickering muscle at his jaw.

The door was opened for her by the time she reached the car, and Hope kept her silence as Luc manoeuvred it around and back through the narrow lane. And while her thoughts should be on the nomination, she couldn't shake Luc from her thoughts as the brooding Italian navigated the London streets with a calm, serene ease.

'You didn't like it,' she observed.

'Like what?'

'Back at the shoot. The attention?'

'No.' The word was clipped and should have ended the conversation.

Hope frowned. 'Can I ask why?'

For a moment she thought he might not answer.

'It's not real,' he said with a shrug. 'It's not me that they are attracted to. It's what I look like.'

And the smile dropped from Hope's lips, startled by the fact that this particular sentiment linked them in a way that made her think he might have understood that about her too.

Before she could pursue the conversation, he pulled into the car lane in front of Harcourts and she couldn't believe her eyes. There was a crowd of paparazzi spilling from the pavement into the road.

'We should use the underground garage,' Luc insisted.

'They've already seen us,' she replied, angry that her cousin had managed to turn everything into a circus. She was the one who was supposed to control the media, but PR and Marketing were two different departments.

'There are too many people out there.'

'If you won't let me out here,' she said, reaching for the door, 'then I'll do it my—'

'Don't!'

The natural authority in his tone, the sense of irrefutable command, held her so still that she didn't move until he opened the door for her. Furious with him for his authoritarian streak and herself for obeying, she got out of the car, refusing to spare him a glance.

But she was unprepared for the sudden press of people around her. Hope was jostled to the side before Luc could reach her and, tipped off-balance, she landed awkwardly. Suddenly she felt an ice-cold slap across her chest and heard the collective gasp from hundreds of journalists who had caught the moment that someone had knocked iced coffee across her cream cashmere top.

She was still reeling, not just from the spill but the sheer volume of paparazzi, when Luc pulled her against him and tucked her under his arm. He escorted her singlehandedly through the throng and into the foyer of Harcourts.

It was all too much. The flashbulbs, the sticky ice-cold liquid soaking into the fine wool, the heat of Luc's body and the way he just…protected her. He didn't stop in the marble foyer, instead pressing them forward, through to the staff-only area and the staff lifts where, thankfully, one had just arrived.

* * *

Luca ushered Hope inside the lift and slammed a palm on the buttons to close the doors before she could even speak. She looked up at him, horror, anger, shock and fury all vying for dominance, and cursed. Loud and furiously. Luca watched as she turned to the mirror lining the back of the lift and took in her ruined top.

'Are you okay?' he demanded.

She was staring at herself, the obvious damp stain spreading down her chest and across her stomach. Angrily, she pulled the ruined cashmere from her waistband.

'Hey!' Luca said, louder, grabbing her shoulders and pulling her around to face him. 'Are you okay?'

'No, of course I'm not okay,' she replied, gesturing to her top.

'That's what you're worried about right now?' he said, wrestling his anger under control. He reached behind him to pull the stop button on the lift. The lights shifted from bright to a standby glow, casting them both in shadow.

'No, Luc. What I'm worried about right now is Harcourts. This means something to me. If I'm to go in there and put my support behind someone other than Simon then I can't do it looking like I've just crawled out of a garbage bin!'

She spun round, turning her back to him, clearly trying, and failing, to get her emotions under control. She shook her head. 'This company, this business, my family—they all deserve better than Simon Harcourt.'

In the reflection, he saw how her chest rose and fell with the sheer power of her anger. And then, when she caught his gaze in the mirrored wall, anger morphed into a heat that frayed the edges of his resistance to her. He braced against the way that her hungry gaze flicked down to his jaw and back. He slammed his eyes closed, hoping to sever the intimate connection he felt stirring in him when she looked at him like that.

Get. Your. Head. On. Straight.

He forced himself to think practically about what she needed. Her ruined sweater. Appearance was important to her—not through vanity, he knew, but as a tool.

'Do you have time to get something from the store?'

'Not now,' she replied. 'The press outside held us up.'

Frustration at the entire situation made his movements harsh and stiff. He flicked the button of his suit jacket and shrugged out of it, dropping it on the floor beside him.

Hope watched him with large round eyes.

'What are you—'

Her words were cut off when his fingers reached to yank his tie loose, as he drew one silk strip from the other, pulling it from his neck and casting it aside onto his jacket. He angled his head slightly to flick the button at his neck and started on the next when she held up her hands between them.

'Stop! What are you doing?'

Despite her words, her hungry gaze was locked onto the progress his hands had made, and damn if that didn't send a thrill straight to his groin. He ignored her and the way his pulse pounded through his veins and his stomach tightened, tugging the shirt from his waistband.

He wished he couldn't see the naked desire in her gaze dancing through her confusion. It was wrong—inappropriate—and somehow that only turned the screw tightening his arousal. For someone who spent his life watching others, the feel of her gaze on him was like a weight, pressing against all the places she was looking. Pressing *hard*.

'You need something to wear,' he said, his voice like gravel, shrugging out of the sleeves and passing his shirt to her.

And, just like that, he felt her attention slam against his entire body. He felt it as she took in the breadth of his chest and shoulders, the musculature of his arms, the flare of surprise at the tattoo that wrapped around his bicep and disappeared beneath the white vest tucked into his suit trousers.

His skin was branded by the heat of her gaze, flames licking across his body burning hotter than he'd experienced before. His blood was thick in his veins, making every part of his body hot and heavy. He wasn't into self-delusion. He knew what this was. He knew how dangerous it was. And that single thought sliced through the heat connecting him to her.

He pressed the shirt she still hadn't taken towards her again and Hope blinked.

* * *

Hope was glad he hadn't spoken again because she wasn't sure she'd have heard him through the blood rushing in her ears. She took the shirt, still warm from his body, and he turned so that his back was to her. His head was bowed and she realised that he was both giving her privacy and protecting her modesty.

Jesus. Where had her modesty been when she'd been utterly undone by just the way he'd taken off his shirt? If he'd taken even a minute more she might have done something stupid, like reach for him.

The tattoo decorating his bicep...a horse's flank disappeared beneath his vest and she saw feathers in black and white detail that made her think of winged horses and gods.

Pegasus.

Luc cleared his throat and she realised he was prompting her again. Embarrassment burned her cheeks and she turned her back on him. She pulled the soaked cashmere top from her body and threw it aside.

In the mirror she caught sight of their reflections and her breath caught. They stood back to back. Luc tall, tanned skin, white vest glowing in the half-light, breath expanding his chest, stretching that cotton across muscles that made her weak. And her, dark trousers almost a match for his, skin pale and her nude bra making them look like...like...

She bit her lip to stop herself from betraying the kaleidoscope of erotic images twisting into her mind. Luc's head jerked as if he'd sensed it somehow, but he didn't turn to look. But that he'd fought the need to look burned a desire she had never experienced before deep into her chest.

No. She had to stop this. He worked for her, she warned herself. He was her subordinate and she couldn't… Something about that thought snagged and stirred. Because the one thing that had become so clear in her mind was that there was nothing subordinate about Luc. She shrugged into his white shirt, and immediately the scent of him that enveloped her pulled at her thoughts. It was expensive, the cologne. Too expensive for a chauffeur.

She filtered through the possibilities and as she began to bring her conclusions together, quick, determined fingers threaded buttons through holes and sharp, efficient movements tucked the shirt beneath her waistband.

She turned to the mirror, pulled a little at the shirt to ensure that it sat right and refused to look Luc in the eye as she leaned to press the button to release the hold on the lift and braced as it jerked back into life.

Heat burned her cheeks as she thought how foolish, how stupid she had been not to see it sooner. She'd been taken in once again, and she cursed herself for not learning the lesson that had already cost her too much.

Luc frowned, as if sensing the change in her. He bent to pick up his jacket from the floor and shoved his tie in his pocket and Hope hated herself for the desperate hunger that somehow surpassed her anger.

The lift opened out onto her floor and they both

ignored the stares following them as they made their way to her office in silence. And she realised in a heartbeat that *he* was leading *her*. It had happened that quickly. He had assumed control, *just like that*.

He walked straight over to the large window, probably drawn by the impressive view of Hyde Park. She didn't really care, as long as it put space between them. She waited until he turned towards her, a small power play she so desperately needed in that moment.

He stood there, hands in pockets, his black suit jacket over a vest, looking so damn gorgeous it made her knees tremble. Anger, she told herself, lied to herself. That was what she was feeling. Fury, even.

'You're not a chauffeur, are you?' It was less a question than a statement.

He inhaled and squared his shoulders, and stood tall, as if pulling himself to his full height. It only made him seem *larger*, more *him*. As if he'd shed a false persona before answering.

'No.'

She clenched her fists, bracing against the hurt and anger crashing through her.

'Security?' she asked, remembering the way he'd protected her.

'Yes.'

'My brother?'

Luc nodded.

'Hope? The meeting is about to start,' Elise said gently from the doorway, as if she knew she was interrupting.

Hope glared at Luc. 'Stay here,' she ordered, even though she wasn't sure she still had the right to do so.

* * *

She hurried down the corridors that took her from the old wing towards the meeting room where the shareholders had gathered to decide a future they barely had any interest in, so angry she wanted to cry. But she couldn't afford to think about Luc and Nate and how betrayed she felt that her brother thought so little of her. The nomination. That was all that mattered in this moment, and she shoved any other thoughts aside. She walked into the meeting room and a staff member closed the door behind her.

Simon was standing beside her grandfather and, *oh, God*, she was so sick of the power moves and game playing.

'We've been waiting—'

'Then let's get on with it,' she interrupted, drawing a few surprised glances her way.

She went to her assigned seat, to the left-hand side of the Chairman, and sat down, her teeth clenched together so hard her jaw ached.

'We have a nomination for Simon Harcourt,' her grandfather informed the room.

Hope waited for a counter-nomination, looking out across the faces of the thirty or so board members, none of whom met her eye. They might have voted for Nate but without him here, no one would stand against Simon. Her stomach clenched and her heart plummeted.

The silence was deafening and she was sure that everyone in the room could hear the dull thud of her heartbeat. *No, no, no.* This couldn't be happening. She wasn't enough. She couldn't do it, not by herself.

'Are there any other nominations?'

Her breath, locked in her chest, felt like a bomb that was about to explode.

You can't sit on the fence any more, Hope.

'If not, then we will forgo the vote and—'

'Me.' The word burst from her lips. 'I nominate myself.'

CHAPTER FOUR

LUCA PACED THE breadth of the room, furious with himself. On the one hand, now that Hope knew who he was, it would make it easier to protect her. On the other hand, he had never dropped the ball so hard before in his life. His company's future was on the line, for heaven's sake. A contract that would launch him light years ahead of any expectations he'd had for Pegaso. So he needed to get his head out of fantasies of Hope Harcourt and back on track. He was about to start another lap of the room when he heard the click of her heels on the parquet flooring outside the office.

He turned expectantly. 'That was quick.'

She threw a folder onto her desk and glared at him. 'You're fired.'

Luca accepted her response as his due, but still shook his head slowly. 'You didn't hire me.'

She held his gaze for a beat before producing her mobile from her pocket. His guess was that she was trying to reach Nate. And if she could get through? Brilliant. Luca had a few choice things he wanted to say to his client. But, unfortunately for both of them, Nate didn't answer.

'You need protection,' Luca warned her as she hung up the phone.

'*If* I need it, I can get it for myself.'

'But you haven't.'

She glared at him again, before turning her back to him to throw her phone on the desk. He gave her the time to gather herself. A lot had happened in a very short space of time.

'Luc?' she asked, without turning.

'Luc*a*,' he corrected. 'Luca Calvino.'

He saw the line of tension across her shoulders, the grip of her hands on the table. He could only imagine the sense of betrayal she must be feeling, but that wasn't his job, nor his responsibility, he argued. Nate was his client, not her.

'The meeting?' he asked.

'Do you care?'

Her question nudged at his conscience. 'For professional purposes,' he lied.

'Well, I've pissed off three-quarters of the board, my grandfather and my cousin. Though, admittedly, I'm not too crushed by the last one. Apparently, they wanted to give Simon the easy win, celebrate over the weekend and resume work as normal on Monday.'

She turned back to him, her cheeks a little pink, her eyes glittering angrily. 'You're not just a bodyguard,' she accused.

'CEO. Pegaso Securities.'

Her gaze flew to his shoulder, as if she were seeing his tattoo beneath the layers of his clothing.

Focus. Hope's protection. His future contract.

'I'm not going anywhere,' he warned, 'so you might as well use me properly, rather than as just your driver.'

Hope let out a laugh that seemed far too cynical for her. 'You're not driving me anywhere ever again, Calvino.'

He levelled her with a gaze that pretty much said, *Think again.*

'I. Don't. Need. You,' she spelled out. 'I can handle it myself.'

'Of course you can,' he replied without missing a beat, his agreement clearly taking her by surprise. 'You can court shareholders; you can make your deals. I'm not interfering with that, but what you can't do is all of that *and* watch your back.'

She turned, her hands anchored on the desk behind her, and he fought the urge to look away as his shirt pulled tight across her chest. Now was not the time for errant thoughts.

'And what is it I have to watch my back for? Journalists with cups of coffee?' she replied, her tone full of scorn.

'Your cousin is mounting a coup. And it seems his weapon of choice is the press.'

Hope rolled her eyes and he ignored it, stepping closer to her to emphasise his point. Her eyes turned to him, flashing warning signs he also ignored. She needed to hear this.

'Every single time you challenge him, a story comes out. Every single time he feels slighted, a new series of articles comes into the press.'

'It's a coincidence. I'm in the public spotlight. I have to be, for my job.'

Luca shook his head. 'It's not. When you argued against him moving the Harcourt brand manufacturing factory to cut costs, the next day the headlines were about you snubbing an invitation from the royal family.'

'There *was* no invitation.'

'When you argued against the change in staff hours, the headlines the next day were about you firing a designer.'

'He went on paternity leave.'

'And when you stopped him from switching transportation contacts, this happened,' he said, showing her the screen of his phone.

'That was…' She trailed off, looking at the newspaper headline he'd pulled up. 'He couldn't have had anything to do with Martin. That was different… It was…'

'Personal? You think your cousin is above that? Your engagement had been broken for six months by that point. Why would the papers suddenly be interested in digging it up then?'

'Because I'd been out with friends?'

'Such a rare occasion that it demands a hit piece about how you broke the heart of your fiancé, when we all know that what really happened was—'

'I was there, I don't need reminding of what happened,' she yelled at him. She ran her hand across her forehead, as if thinking through his accusation.

'The journalist? Just happened to be at Oxford with Simon. Same year, same social circle, and a rather invested interest in any scandal related to you.'

She started to pace the room, just as he had done earlier. She shook her head. 'I didn't see it. I always thought it was just normal unhealthy interest, but not targeted in *that* way.' She shook her head again, as if trying to refute it, but Luca needed to press his point home now.

'Right now, you need to focus on the vote next week, so I'm going to focus on what you don't have the capacity to do.'

'I could hire my own security,' she said, repeating her earlier threat.

'You could, but you won't. Why?' he asked, before answering his own question. 'Because you need to figure out how you're going to win the vote. And that starts with what happens at the Harcourts Winter Party at the opera tomorrow night.'

Understanding and realisation dawned in her eyes. She knew he was right. Luca was now ninety-nine percent sure he had her. And *finally* he could actually do the job the way he wanted.

'And what do you get out of it?' she asked, catching him by surprise.

'What do you mean?'

'A CEO doesn't usually get this hands-on, even for a client like Nathanial Harcourt,' she said, a dangerous glint in her eye. 'I want to know what makes me—*this*—so special?' she demanded.

'Hope—'

'What are you getting out of this, Luca?' she demanded, and he hated how it looked. How whatever had passed between them—and something *had* passed between them—would be tainted by this.

She held his gaze steadily until he answered.

'The global security contract for Harcourts.'

Even braced for his response, she blanched. 'He had no right to do that,' she argued.

'Perhaps,' he agreed, trying to ignore the fact that he suddenly felt like a bastard. 'But really? Right now? That's not what's important. Look, forget your brother. Forget who's paying the bill. Forget what happens next. I'm here,' he said, taking another step towards her. 'And I'm good. I'm *very* good. Let me do my job.'

He held his breath. And he wondered if, for a minute, she was doing exactly the same.

'Fine,' she said, turning to walk around to her seat behind the desk.

He breathed and nodded. 'I'll be outside when you are ready to leave. Am I taking you home?' he asked.

'Where else would you take me?' she asked, the ice in her tone freezing him to the bone. But the words— he couldn't keep them back, even if he tried.

'To your grandfather's? A friend's? You shouldn't be alone tonight.'

'There are a lot of things I shouldn't be tonight.

But that is neither any of your business nor anything to do with my protection.'

Chastised, with lines redrawn, Luca Calvino left her office.

The next evening, as Hope got ready for the Harcourts Christmas party, held each year at the Royal Opera House, she wrestled the feelings oscillating danger- ously between anger and humiliation. Betrayal and a sense of her own stupidity. A part of her desperately wanted to cancel, but now that she had thrown her hat in the ring as the new CEO, she *had* to be there.

Luc had driven her home in stony silence last night.

No. Not Luc.

Luca, she corrected. Luc had been a handsome Italian chauffeur she'd had a silly feminine reaction to. *Luca* was a billionaire businessman whose only interest in her was an international contract with Har- courts and nothing more.

She'd praised herself for having enough self-control to at least wait until she'd got home before doing a search on him, although the fallout from putting her- self forward for the CEO position meant she had more than enough to deal with. It was actually a testament to Simon's popularity that only a third of the board 'popped by' her office to show their support. Of that third, she was probably only guaranteed half of those votes, the others just doing it for show.

But, finally at home, she'd not been able to stop herself. With a large glass of Tempranillo, she'd

typed his name into the search engine and found...
very little. There was a single photograph from a
few years ago on his bio, and she'd had to squint to
make sure that it was, in fact, him. There was little to
no personal information and therefore no way to see
whether he'd been telling her the truth about growing
up in Palizzi. She didn't know why, but it had become
important that at least one piece of what he'd told her
had been real. Even if it was just that. But not knowing only added to her feeling of insecurity.

Because she'd done it again, hadn't she? Seen and
read too much into something, some*one*, who was
only out for themselves. She looked at her reflection
in the mirror-lined lift of her apartment building and
found it hard to feel anything other than disdain for
the woman staring back at her. After Martin, she'd
promised herself she'd learnt that lesson, but clearly
she hadn't.

When her phone had rung last night with Nate's
name appearing on the screen, she hadn't been able to
answer it. Even though she'd wanted to speak to him,
even though she *should* have. But she hadn't. Because
he'd not trusted her. He'd not thought she was strong
enough to handle things, so he'd gone behind her
back. Just like the way he'd done with her ex-fiancé.

And if Nate didn't think she could handle that,
what would he think when he found out she'd put
herself forward as CEO? He'd probably think it was
nothing short of laughable. Even though she had two
degrees in business and marketing and had just as
much family knowledge as either of them.

She'd never be able to get away from the fact that her father had always wanted Nate to have Harcourts. For his son to take the lead of the family business and that thought, last night, of all nights, had hurt.

Hope bit her lip as she emerged from her apartment to find Luca waiting for her beside the open car door as if nothing had changed between them. And then she remembered that, for him, nothing had.

Forcing down her feelings, Hope got into the car and smoothed the black silk skirt of the haute couture dress one of the designers exclusive to Harcourts had made for her. Wide-strapped V-neck panels were flattering and tight over her top half, and the layered high/low skirt provided drama and a hint of sex appeal. Not enough to scare off the shareholders attending the Harcourts Winter Party, she had ensured. But enough to remind herself that she was still a desirable woman in her own right. A reminder she needed very much in that moment, with the weight of Luca's gaze on her.

As she studiously ignored him, she considered the night ahead. The party was a tradition started nearly one hundred years ago. On the second Saturday in January, Harcourts would hire the ROH for a night to delight the staff and their families. Its success had been replicated across their international locations and, although the Sydney Opera House was magnificent, this had always been her favourite. And she used that memory to ground her, used the strength of her feelings for Harcourts to give her the focus she needed. Tonight was about making the connections she needed to beat Simon and now, more than ever, that had become vital.

'We're here.'

'Thank you,' she replied automatically, ruthlessly relegating Luca to someone of no more importance than any other member of staff.

Hope checked her reflection in the mirror one last time, unable to afford any smudged make-up or any more photo disasters. That morning's headlines had been a montage of various images of her horrified face and some very unnecessary close-ups of her chest.

Luca opened her door and, ignoring the goosebumps that flashed over her skin from his proximity, she stepped out onto the red carpet, a touch of glamour that the staff appreciated. Photographers and journalists waiting for a glimpse of one of the most prestigious business events of the year were kept at bay by a rope and various security staff. She looked ahead through the glass-fronted entrance to see her grandfather surrounded by a group of tuxedoed men and their wives in impressive ballgowns.

Hope braced herself. She was used to arriving alone to these kinds of affairs—having learned a long time ago that it was better to spare both her date and the press the kind of speculation that followed—but somehow, after what had passed between her and Luca, she felt it more acutely. Leaving him in her wake, she smiled at the press, made a joke about no one having any iced coffee, at which most laughed, and made her way into the foyer of the Royal Opera House.

Smiles greeted her, as many fake as real, and she mingled with the shareholders and their partners for a drink or two before they heard the five-minute curtain call. Once again, that dip in her stomach returned. Tonight would be the first time that she'd be alone in the family box.

Her grandfather had his own, Simon's side of the family would be in another. Usually, she'd be here with Nate and they'd spend the evening gossiping about the board members and their snooty behaviour. But Nate was still recuperating and she would have to bear the attention alone.

As people started to peel off for their respective seats, she caught her grandfather's eye and thought for a second that she saw understanding and compassion in his gaze. But she knew better. Smile bright and eyes glittering, she made her way along the red-carpeted staircase to the door that opened onto the private box that she remembered from her childhood. She walked in and stopped just behind the seats, cast in shadow, watching the auditorium fill with Harcourts' staff and friends and family.

The noise rose up from below, gentle chatter, a laugh punctuating the hum. She wished the excitement was infectious enough to distract her, but it wasn't. Directly opposite her box, on the other side of the stalls, Simon gently slapped his father on the back, whilst scanning the auditorium. He looked up and found her watching him. She clearly wasn't as well hidden as she'd thought. He nodded in acknowledgement, the civility of it making Hope angry, until he purposely cut the connection to look at someone in the stalls below. Curious, she followed his gaze, and her fingers tightened to white as she fisted the evening's programme.

'What is Martin de Savoir doing here?'

The question made Hope jump and the sting of adrenaline pricked at her skin as she pressed a hand to her chest.

'Don't turn around,' Luca commanded. 'I'd rather people not know I'm here.'

Hope huffed out a bitter laugh. 'How novel. Someone who *doesn't* want to be seen with me. What are you doing here?' she demanded in a harsh whisper.

'My job,' Luca replied tightly.

He'd spent three hours that afternoon familiarising himself with the ROH layout and communicating with their security, before clearing a suspicious package sent to Hope's office that turned out to be flowers congratulating her on the nomination. It had been a miracle that he'd made it to Hope's apartment on time. And while he bore the lion's share of the responsibility for her animosity towards him, dealing with their acidic interactions was something he could do without.

From the shadows at the back of the box, he peered down into the auditorium to see Hope's ex-fiancé smack in the middle of the stalls, halfway between her and Simon Harcourt.

'Do you know who he's with?' Luca asked. *He* knew, he just wasn't sure how up-to-date Hope was on her ex's love life and what it would cost her to hear it.

He watched as Hope purposefully turned her attention away from the lower level to scan the rest of the auditorium. He imagined that she had a practically perfect smile on those incendiary red lips he'd caught sight of in the rear-view mirror of the car earlier. He was sure she'd been aiming for elegant rather than downright carnal, but anyone looking at the perfect bow of her lips painted in fire engine red would have to have been dead from the neck down not to think wicked thoughts.

'That is Imogen Frotheram.'

'That's quite a mouthful,' he observed, peering at the young blonde woman who looked remarkably like Hope.

'Twenty-four years old, with an inheritance of nearly one million pounds, and presently engaged to Martin de Savoir,' Hope informed him in a dispassionate tone.

Luca caught Imogen casting a look between her fiancé and up at Hope in the grand tier box, suggesting that perhaps she was only just becoming aware of what she had been drawn into.

'De Savoir doesn't work for Harcourts,' he said, his tone dark with suspicion.

'No,' Hope replied, still looking out as the remaining guests began to take their seats. She even waved at someone in the stalls.

'Then how did he get a ticket?'

There was barely a pause before she replied. 'That area is reserved for Simon's friends and family.'

Although her voice was carefully level, he could only imagine the fury that she must be feeling. To have her ex-fiancé here, with his new fiancée? The day *after* she'd gone head-to-head with her cousin? Simon was trying to get at her, undermining her on every level he could, publicly in front of the shareholders. And doing it all without even getting his hands dirty.

Hope moved forward to take her seat, the voluminous skirt swaying with her hips in a way that made him want to bracket her waist in his palms. *Graceful.* It caught his attention when he should have been thinking of so much more.

'Do you like opera, Luca?' she asked, holding the programme in front of her mouth to disguise their conversation.

'I do.'

She cocked her head to one side as if surprised, and he smiled.

'It's a national crime not to adore Puccini.'

'And Turandot?' she asked.

'One of my favourites,' he admitted begrudgingly of the opera famous, mostly, for the song Nessun Dorma.

'Really?' This time Hope had been unable to hide the surprise from her voice. 'I didn't picture you as a romantic.'

Luca clenched his jaw so hard he nearly broke a tooth in order not to ask, to demand, how she had been picturing him. The silence screamed between them and he was about to say something when the conductor tapped his baton to ready the orchestra.

The entire way through the first act he tried to keep his focus on his surroundings, but Hope was more distracting than the dramatic death of the Prince of Persia.

Hope. One of the answers to the three questions Turandot asks of her suitors. Should they answer incorrectly, they are put to death. Only the one who answers each of the riddles can become her husband. He wondered what Hope made of the heroine so angered by the assault on her ancestor, she sets about taking revenge on all of her would-be suitors.

From where he was standing, tucked into the rich red velvet curtain enveloped by shadows, he could see the delicate lines of her shoulders and neck. Hope's blonde hair was looped into an elaborate twist, held in place by a gold hairpin, leaving her long slender neck bare and begging to be caressed. The V on the front of her dress was mirrored at the back and the dim lighting played in shadows across her shoulder blades and spine. Instinctively, his hand flexed before he fisted it and shoved it behind his back.

He usually had more control over himself than this, but he had to admit he'd never encountered anyone like Hope before. His mind returned to his earlier conversation with Nathanial Harcourt. He'd expected a fight on his hands, to keep the contract, to keep their agreement, but Nate had seemed distracted.

'It's fine. As long as she's safe, that's all that mat-

ters.' The Englishman's voice had sounded strained,
but Luca knew that he wouldn't appreciate any show
of concern. 'Keep me informed,' was all he'd said before severing the call. He doubted her brother would
have been so accepting if he'd had any idea of the
erotic desires she evoked in Luca.

As the curtain dropped on the first intermission,
Hope took a moment to gather herself. She hadn't
seen a single second of the opera that was a favourite
of hers too. Instead, the entire time, she'd been aware
only of Luca. Of the weight of his presence, hidden
in the corner, like a protection she both wanted and
hated at the same time.

Shaking off the thought, she needed to get out to the
main foyer. Intermissions were an important part of
social networking and while she'd always begged off
in the past, it was no longer a luxury she could afford.
Standing from her seat, she turned, unable to stop her
gaze flying straight to where Luca was standing—and
instantly wished she hadn't. She'd been so focused on
ignoring him earlier when he was with the car that she
hadn't really taken him in. But now?

If he'd looked good in a suit and tie, Luca Calvino
in a tuxedo was devastating. She wanted to press a
hand to her stomach like some Victorian miss, for the
first time truly understanding that flip in her core.
Deep in her core. Her lips parted on nothing but air
and she didn't miss the way that his gaze flickered
between her mouth and her eyes. She was about to
say something when there was a knock on the door.

Luca's brow dropped in question and Hope, understanding, shook her head to convey that she wasn't expecting anyone. She crossed to the door, gently batting aside Luca's raised hand warning her to stop, and opened it, regretting it instantly.

Her ex-fiancé lounged against the frame as if he had come to charm her rather than taunt her. Burying her anger deep, she waited. She had learned long ago that nothing frustrated Martin more than having to do things for himself.

'Not going to invite me in?'

'No,' she said, keeping her tone neutral and her expression purposely bland.

The wave of anger she felt coming from where Luca stood in the shadows heated her skin like a fierce caress. But all it did was make her aware that he was seeing this. Seeing that *this* was the man she'd nearly married. Shame and anger licked at her like flames.

Several guests passed in the hallway, casting them curious glances, clearly aware of the history between them and already beginning to gossip. Just as—she imagined—he'd planned.

'Don't you want to know why I'm here?' Martin taunted.

'No.'

'Even if I had something that you might want?' he leered.

'You have *nothing* I want, Martin. I promise you that,' she said, struggling to keep herself calm. He peeled himself angrily from the door frame and stood there glaring at her.

'Everyone wants something, Hope. Sadly, I was never going to give you what you are so desperate for,' he said, with so much false sincerity it curdled her stomach.

'And what was that?' she asked before she could stop herself.

'Love,' he whispered meanly, leaning into her ear.

She slammed the door on him, hating that she could hear his taunting laugh as he walked away.

Luca hadn't made out Martin's reply, but it took nearly everything in him not to wrench the door open and go after the bastard. What on earth was wrong with these people? No, his own wasn't exactly the perfect nuclear family. He didn't know and didn't care to know his father, he barely saw his mother—only when she deemed it safe and secret enough, but this?

Vipers.

It was a description Nate had used too and it barely touched the surface.

Hope stood facing the door she had just slammed shut, the rapid breaths pressing against the black satin crossed over her chest. She was looking down, that curved line of her neck bent. Until she rolled her shoulders and straightened her back and he watched as Hope rebuilt her armour, brick by brick, thought by thought.

'Can you get the car?'

'*Sì,*' he replied, unaware that his emotions were

riding him hard enough for him to answer in his native Italian.

'Have it ready in five minutes.'

'*Sì,*' he said. Before he left, he marvelled as she resumed her seat in the private box. And just before the curtain rose on Turandot's second act, she even smiled and waved to some of the staff who caught her eye, looking for all the world as if nothing had happened.

What had Martin said to her?

The question become an urgent refrain as he made his way from the theatre to the garage where the car was. Luca barely breathed until he had the car at the entrance to the Royal Opera House and saw Hope making her way towards him.

Head high, back straight and as poised and regal as a queen, sophistication and class dripped from every pore and no one would have guessed that she had just been emotionally eviscerated by her ex-fiancé. Luca exited the car without taking his eyes off her and, reaching for her door, he held it open and closed it behind her.

He wasn't sure what made him look back at that moment but, when he did, he saw Simon Harcourt standing at a second-floor window with an inscrutable expression on his face.

CHAPTER FIVE

HOPE WAS BARELY holding on. All she wanted to do was get back to her apartment, take this wretched dress off, wipe off the make-up and… No. She wouldn't cry. She wouldn't give in. Martin had been purposely baiting her. Distracting her. He'd done what he'd set out to achieve—what *Simon* had set out to achieve, that was. Instead of making the rounds at intermission and forging valuable connections, she'd remained in the opera box and had run away at the first chance.

When would she stop being such a fool? She *had* to be better than this. Cleverer. But all she could think— hear—was his parting words to her on a loop.

'I was never going to give you what you are so desperate for.'

She hated him. Hated that he was right.

As the car arrived at her apartment block she felt Luca's curiosity pressing against her, filling the car, suffocating her. The moment they pulled to a stop, she flung the door open and fled, desperate to es- cape. She didn't want him to know. Didn't want him to have any part of her. Not when she couldn't trust that he wasn't just the same as Martin.

As she pushed through the revolving doors, she felt him fall into step a little way behind her and though she wanted to tell him to leave, to stop following her, she didn't trust herself to speak.

The doors were open on the lift when she reached it and Hope tapped the button for her floor again and again to close them. She needed him to stop. She needed to be alone. To lick her wounds. To hurt. She turned back in time to see him pound a fist against the wall as the doors closed, cutting them off.

She sucked in a lungful of air, willing back the tears and trying to ease the pressure on her chest, thankful for the reprieve from Luca's constant attention. He saw and knew too much. She shook her head at herself, gathering the shreds of her dignity, and got out of the lift.

Her thumb was on the access pad to her apartment door when Luca came stalking down the corridor. He must have run up the flights of stairs. She turned in the doorway, refusing to let him over the threshold.

'Go away,' she commanded.

He pulled up opposite her, studying her with an intensity she felt tripping over her sensitised skin, pulling at her core, at what made her a woman and what she, as a woman, wanted. There were questions in his eyes, dark and angry. His gaze fastened on hers as if he was willing himself not to look anywhere else on her body and that annoyed her as much as it relieved.

A muscle pulsed at his jaw and it seemed he was as on edge as she was.

'No.'

'No?'

He shook his head. 'I won't go away. Not until I know you're okay.'

Hope huffed out a bitter laugh. 'I am fine. Just another day in the life of Hope Harcourt.'

He looked over her shoulder at the sliver of apartment he could see through the open door and looked back at her. It was all the warning she got.

'No, wait—'

He slipped past her before she could do anything.

'Luca!' she gasped, outraged that he was in her home. 'What do you think you're doing?' she demanded.

He stalked through her apartment like a jungle cat, peering into the rooms with a dispassion that was nearly offensive.

'My job,' he growled, and she wanted to growl right back. She was getting sick of hearing those two words. She didn't want him to be doing his job, she didn't want him here because he *had* to be. If he and her brother hadn't lied to her, she wouldn't be in this mess, feeling one thing and wanting another.

Luca turned, feeling Hope's frustration roll off her in waves. Good. He wanted her frustrated, he wanted her angry. Anything was better than the pain and hurt he'd seen hidden deep only moments before.

He caught sight of a wine fridge in the corner of the neat kitchen that opened onto the dining room. 'Drink?'

'Excuse me?' Hope demanded, a red flash across her cheeks.

'Would you like a drink?'

'You're offering me a drink in my own home?' She stared at him as if it were the greatest breach of etiquette she'd ever seen.

'I know I could do with one,' he bit out under his breath as he crossed to the kitchen. Hope's apartment was exactly as he had imagined—not that it was hard, having reviewed the floor plans and the original sales brochure. He probably knew more about her apartment than she did. He bent down to the wine fridge and scanned the labels. What he really wanted was to know what Martin had said to her. Instinctively, Luca knew it was important. Really important.

'I don't know what you think you saw tonight—'

'What I saw,' he interrupted as he pulled a very decent white from the fridge, 'was a vile, objectionable man using social pressure to keep you in your place while he tried to emotionally manipulate you.'

He reached for two wine glasses from the shelf above the countertop, liking the ergonomic feel of the apartment; everything was in reach where it should be, or was expected to be.

'Did he do that while you were together?' he asked, trying to keep the dangerous anger simmering beneath his skin at bay.

He felt the breath she held, the fury she tried to

contain as if it were a living presence between them. He waited out her silence as he poured the pale wine into each glass. He looked to where Hope stood in the middle of her apartment, waiting until she gave up the fight.

She placed her bag and wrap on the arm of the sofa and came to stand with the breakfast bar between them. He slid the glass of wine across the gleaming marble and she took a sip before answering.

'No,' she said, putting the glass back down on the bar. 'No,' she said, shaking her head again. 'He was many things, but he doesn't have the intellect for that kind of emotional manipulation. But he was very good at hiding his true nature. I had absolutely no idea,' she admitted. 'And I should have,' she said, as if admonishing herself.

'We were twelve when our parents died and my grandfather became our guardian. He decided that boarding school was the best place for us and sent my brother to Eton, and me to St Saviour's.' The words became thick on her tongue. 'It was the first time I'd spent even a night away from my brother. As twins, we'd been unusually inseparable and suddenly my parents were gone, my life was upside down and I was alone.'

She turned to the window, perhaps unseeing of the illuminated London nightscape beyond the glass.

'It was…an adjustment. Because of my parents' death, the publicity, the tragedy, the family notoriety, everyone in the school knew who I was. It counted among its number the daughters of dignitaries, ambassadors and even princesses, but I was *famous*,' she said, smiling bitterly.

'I didn't quite realise what that meant until a picture of me trying alcohol for the first time, in a desperate attempt to fit in and find a place in the schoolgirl hierarchy, found its way onto the front page of a daily rag. After that, it was a photo of me getting changed after gym.'

She shrugged, trying to hide how much it had hurt, how much it still hurt, but he could see it. Could tell how much it cost her to remember, to open this up for him, because he'd demanded it. Hope was describing exactly the kind of invasive press attention that his mother had told him she'd been trying to avoid. But with one difference—his mother had only been trying to protect herself. It sounded as if there had been no one to protect Hope. Until it was too late. It struck him then that they each lived on opposite sides of public life—him in the shadows and her in the glare of the spotlight.

'So you'd have thought I'd have learned my lesson by the time I met Martin, but apparently not. At university, things were easier. I was as anonymous as I'd ever been and I let my guard down. I was *wooed* by him and fell for his lies, hook, line and sinker.

'I thought myself in love,' she said, the cynicism dripping from her tone like acid that would only ever harm herself. 'And I would have married him, had my brother not realised he was only after my money.'

Luca didn't miss the way she had tripped over

those words and his chest ached, not from anger but with understanding. He could easily imagine the kind of hurt she had felt.

'I overheard them talking. Nate confronted Martin about a month before our wedding, at a family event in Tunbridge Wells. And, to this day, they don't know I heard them.'

Luca's glass paused midway to his mouth.

'Nate wanted to pay Martin to leave me, but I broke it off before he could. Martin must have hated that. To not have got a penny out of us. I think that's why he threw his lot in with Simon. And that's how I became the "The Cold-Hearted Harcourt", dumping her fiancé weeks before the wedding.'

'Hope—'

'Better that than to be left by the bastard,' she bit out through clenched teeth.

How her brother had ever thought her weak was beyond Luca. He shook his head.

'So now you know,' she said, her eyes shining. 'And now you can leave,' she ordered regally.

He didn't want to leave her alone, but he couldn't be sure that his reasons were purely professional any more. And that alone was enough to tell him that he should. He left his half-drunk wine on the bar and Hope followed him to the door.

He turned. He wanted to say something but the look in her eyes, powerful, angry and determined, warned him against it and only then did he feel it was okay to leave.

* * *

On Sunday evening Luca received a message from Elise, letting him know that Hope was working from home the next day. And the day after that. During that time, the press made Martin's approach to Hope at the opera into a secret assignation, a fight between jealous ex-lovers, and everything but a plot to dethrone the King. His mother's film also grossed millions at the Hollywood box office and there was something jarring about seeing both of their names in the same newspaper that put Luca in the foulest of moods.

And that was before he received the email about Austria. He picked up his phone and pressed the dial button before he'd even finished reading it.

'What's in Austria?' he demanded.

'Sun, ski and *après-ski*,' Elise replied dreamily, unconcerned by the growl in his voice.

'Clearly. What is she *doing* there?'

'You could ask me *really* nicely...' Hope's assistant drew out, 'but even then, I wouldn't tell you.'

'And this is where she intends to stay?' he asked, scanning and dismissing an image of the large central hotel, with so many access points it was nothing short of a security disaster waiting to happen.

'It's where she usually stays. Angelique has a chalet within the same village and they always go there and they always have so much fun and I'm always *so* jealous.'

The words poured from Hope's assistant so quickly, he barely managed to get the gist of it.

'And if we needed to change the location?'

'I wouldn't recommend it. Hope wouldn't like it one bit.'

Luca stared at the screen, thinking that it would be the least of what she didn't like about him at that point and reminded himself that it was probably not a bad thing either.

The next day Luca was already on the private jet when Hope entered the cabin of the small craft. Her glasses this time were almost completely opaque, leaving him clueless about her reaction to him.

Outwardly, she seemed not to spare him a glance as she took a seat at the furthest end of the cabin, on the opposite side, with her back to him. He smiled inwardly, having expected nothing less, before his conscience stirred. Yes, she was mad at him and she had good reason to be.

He had breached professional lines on the night of the opera. He might have told himself he had good reason, but it still had the same outcome. They were on rocky ground and he needed to get back to solid, professional. He couldn't lose the future contract with Harcourts. It was what he had been working towards for the last ten years.

The air steward came to settle Hope into her seat, asking if she wanted anything to drink before take-off. She kept her voice low, making him strain to hear her, making him work for it. He respected it as much as it frustrated him.

Her phone vibrated with a call and as she held up the screen, he realised he could see it from this angle.

Not that he needed to. The sound of the video call cut through the quiet of the cabin.

'Darling! Tell me you're on your way,' came the cooing voice of a brunette with bright blue eyes.

'Just waiting for take-off.'

'Yes!' The word screamed into the phone and buzzed the speakers harshly.

The laugh Hope allowed herself hit him just as hard.

'So, are you ready to get up to no good?' the brunette demanded.

'Absolutely.'

'Good, because Simon arsehole Harcourt deserves to get sucker punched after all these years.'

Luca frowned, disliking how open the conversation was and very much disliking that he didn't know who the brunette was.

'That he does. I should be there in two hours.'

'The champers is on ice, darling, and I can't wait to see your gorgeous face!'

The switch in atmosphere in the plane the moment Hope disconnected the call was like whiplash, the soft humour severing into serious contemplation, and it reminded him of the time that his mother had been caught by a fan once when she'd been visiting.

At eleven, he was already painfully aware of the need to keep the identity of his mother a secret.

'It's to protect me, Luca. You're doing such a good job protecting me.'

A young woman had nervously approached her idol, asking if she would sign an autograph for her.

'*Of course,*' Anna had said, pushing Luca aside.

He knew the routine by then. He would walk on, just like any other fan who had been dismissed. Usually, he would find the nearest corner, or maybe even just head straight home. But this time he'd watched Anna, how she had lit up, the smile seeming so very genuine, happier even than when she'd been with him only moments before. And he'd felt resentment towards the woman who'd asked for the photograph, jealous that she was the recipient of all that focused joy Anna was capable of when she wanted to be.

Luca shook himself free of the thought. He wasn't usually so preoccupied with thoughts of Anna. In fact, as time had gone on and the visits between them had become more awkward and few and far between, he'd begun to wonder what the point was.

But it was this client. This case. He'd known when Nate had approached him that it would hit a little too close to home, to exactly what he'd spent his life trying to avoid—the press, public scrutiny. And he probably could have argued, after the night at the opera, that someone else would be better suited for her protection detail. But he'd given Nate his word, and that meant something to him.

Hope said her thanks as the air steward placed the espresso beside her and moved off. She'd never thought of the jet as small before, but when so much of her focus was taken up by her awareness of Luca it now seemed almost claustrophobic.

She had been purposely avoiding him since he

had left her apartment that night after the opera. And if she'd thought she could have escaped London and come to Austria without him noticing, she would have. But it seemed that Luca was, indeed, very good at his job.

'Who was that?' he asked from behind her.

She'd have liked to pretend that he'd caught her by surprise, but he hadn't. She'd felt the distance between them getting smaller and smaller with every leap of her pulse. She could try to ignore him for the rest of the trip, but she doubted that she'd have much luck. There was simply no way to ignore Luca Calvino.

'Angelique,' she said on a sigh, wishing that his gravelly voice didn't make her tummy flip in that way.

'You trust her?' he asked, waiting beside the table for her to invite him to sit. Like she'd thought, not that subtle, and not mincing his words today, it seemed.

Locking her gaze on his, direct and unquestionable, 'With my life,' she said honestly. 'I'm sure that you heard the call, and I'm sure that you drew all manner of conclusions about someone who says *champers* and *darling* and who has a chalet in an Austrian ski resort. And you're entitled to draw those conclusions, Luca. But, as I have quite clearly demonstrated to you, I know what it's like to be sold out by someone I deemed a friend. This isn't one of those times and Angelique isn't one of those people.'

'What are we doing in Austria, Hope?' he asked, the bite of exhausted frustration colouring his tone.

She considered whether to tell him the truth. She

didn't like the way that he seemed to take over, without her permission or consultation. So many people did that to her, but with him it seemed all the more important to fight it.

'You have to let me know your plans if I'm going to do my job properly,' he insisted.

'If you need me to tell you my plans, then perhaps you're not up to the job,' she replied tartly.

'It doesn't have to be this difficult.'

'No, you're right. It doesn't. And had I wanted this, rather than you and my brother going behind my back, then it wouldn't be this difficult.'

'That is a very naïve view of the situation,' he said, dismissing her argument. 'It's this simple,' he went on, his index finger tracing an arc on the table. 'Either I'll follow one step behind you, wherever you go, during which time it's entirely possible that a lack of communication could lead to an accidental slip-up, and that the press, who are clearly also following you and looking for a story, will see,' he said with a careless shrug as her ire built and built. 'Or we can work together and make sure that the press see and discover nothing.'

'Are you threatening me?' she demanded.

'I will do whatever I have to do, to get the job done.'

'To get your global contract with Harcourts, you mean.'

Although her verbal jab was little more than a diversionary tactic, it was clear that it meant a lot to her. And he wished he hadn't had his hands tied by her brother, but they had been.

Luca hated the idea that he had to threaten Hope to get her to play ball, and if she'd had any idea that he had absolutely no intention of ever being noticed by the press, she'd have been able to call his bluff. But she didn't. In truth, if he could live in perfect anonymity, Luca would die a happy man. He'd have managed to live his life without ruining his mother's. No matter how large the distance between them, or how difficult the relationship, knowing that his very existence was a constant threat to his mother was a terrible burden to live with. So no, Luca had absolutely no intention of being discovered by the paparazzi, but neither did he have any intention of doing a bad job.

His question hung in the air between them. *What are we doing in Austria?*

'The shareholders don't like me,' she said with a shrug as if she didn't care, even though he doubted that to be true. 'Whether it's the fact I'm a woman, the fact that Nate and I want desperately to take Harcourts into the twenty-first century, or whether I'm not willing to schmooze them in the way they believe they are entitled to. It didn't really matter before now.

'Nate was supposed to be the one who took over the CEO position when Johnson finally stepped down, but clearly we underestimated the deals he'd made with Simon.' She shook her head, as if annoyed with herself. 'Nate had been working on a business deal with Casas Fashion.'

'The Spanish conglomerate?'

'Yes. But something happened and the deal fell through. And before Nate could…he…' She looked out of the window again. 'Well, you know.'

Luca nodded, wondering when Nate had last spoken to his sister. He thought of the Conwarys and how they'd talked around the medical crisis that had struck him down, and realised that there was more than one way to keep a secret.

'Everyone wants something,' she said, repeating words from the mouth of that snake de Savoir, making his hackles rise. 'So I need to give the board something that they want, in order to vote for me and not Simon.'

'And what's that?' he asked.

'An obscene amount of money.'

Clever. Very clever, he thought, satisfaction a shimmering gold in the molten chocolate gaze staring back at him.

'I have to do a deal that will make them forget all their prejudice. Because if avarice is their weakness, it will be my success.'

Hope followed Luca down the stairs from the jet as the luggage was loaded into a sleek, dark SUV with blacked-out windows, her breath misting in the cold air. The private airstrip was in a basin protected by a mountain range on one side and a lake in the distance on the other. The air crisp and cool and promising a snowfall that would be sure to delight the holiday-makers hoping to get in a few last runs before returning their children to school or work after the festive winter break. The runway had been cleared to allow for landing, the snow banked up around the edges looking dirty and industrial, taking just a little of the shine from the alpine fantasy and showing the reality hidden beneath. Something that felt a little too close to home at that moment for Hope.

'Would you like to sit in the front?' Luca asked. She considered it. Thought of the way she'd watch his hands as he steered the wheel, changed gears, the power of it...

'If I sit beside you, the press will want to know who you are.'

It was true, but she still disliked how it forced them back to the roles of employer and employee, even if it wasn't strictly true. Luca's stiff nod in response served to acknowledge as much, as he held the passenger door open for her.

She immediately swiped across the screen of her phone to access her emails. Work. She needed to work, she was *here* to work, and as long as the elaborate scheme she had created with Angelique was a success, she'd meet with her potential business partner that evening and be on her way back home tomorrow, all being well.

Hope had spent two days pulling together the details of what she believed would be the making of Harcourts. Her brother had tried with Casas Industries and while a deal with the Spanish fashion house would have been a solid investment, exciting up to a point, it wouldn't have changed anything. Hope wanted more. Hope wanted bigger. With Sofia Obeid,

Hope was almost sure she had it. And while that familiar part of her wanted to speak to her brother, to ask if she was doing the right thing, if the deal was actually as good as she'd hoped, another—stronger—part wanted to keep this to herself. In case she failed.

She tried to focus on the inbox on her screen, but soon became distracted by the view beyond the window. She had always loved snow-covered mountains. There was a wildness inherent in them that she felt she was never allowed to be. A raw, unmatched, solid force to them that was not action or reaction, push or pull, it just *was*. Simply power, unquestionable and immovable.

Like Luca.

No, she argued with herself. *Like* me. *Like how* I *want to be.*

She watched as the familiar turn-off to the village just outside of Kitzbühel came up on her left…and then disappeared as they passed it.

'Luca, I think we've missed the turning.'

'No, we didn't.'

'Yes,' she said, craning her neck back to where they should have gone. 'We've passed it.'

Her statement was met with silence.

'Luca?' she asked, her tone a warning which was also ignored.

CHAPTER SIX

THE SLAM OF her car door cracked through the snow-heavy silence like a gunshot. A bird erupted from a nearby fir tree, sending a flutter of wings and snow off into the forest just behind the sprawling wooden chalet.

Not even on pain of death would Hope admit that this place looked as if it had been plucked out of her daydreams. Not that Luca seemed to be bothered in any way whether she liked the ski lodge or not. He had hauled open the boot of the car and was removing their meagre luggage and carrying it up the stairs towards the front door, his movements quick, efficient and laced with a controlled impatience.

'You went behind my back,' she accused, following him as he made the trip back to the car. She turned to stare up at the accommodation. It seemed almost wasteful to use it for just a night. She counted the windows along the second floor of the chalet, bracketed by wooden eaves and a balcony. The entire place—built to house at least fifteen, from what she could see—looked as if it belonged in a chocolate advert. The luxurious promise of sweetness, warmth and decadence just behind its doors.

Her mind threw up a marketing campaign just like that—a couple very much in love, sinking to a white fur rug before a roaring fire, mulled wine on one side and seventy percent dark chocolate on the other. The mountains, perhaps a few slopes visible in the distance through an open window.

The slam of the car boot made her jump and Luca stalked past her, refusing to spare her a glance, up the stairs and, after entering a code in the door's keypad, into the chalet. She stamped her boots on the snow-covered driveway, kicking out the cold from her feet, and followed him reluctantly into one of the most beautiful places she'd ever stayed.

The door opened onto a large utility-style hallway, perfect for hanging coats and taking off boots. Along one side was a rack for skis and poles, snowboards and holders for boots and every kind of winter sport that could be imagined. At the end of the utility room was a door that stood partly ajar.

Braced and ready to give Luca a piece of her mind, she swept through the door and...

Oh.

The ground floor was as serene and soothing as any spa. A sauna glowed gently from behind its glass front, the wooden seating and panels promising a bone-deep warmth that Hope suddenly craved more than she could have imagined. On the other side was a hammam, offering a slick, humid heat that reactivated fantasies that she'd desperately wanted to put away. A small pool lay just beyond the bounds of the building, beneath a canopy of fairy lights covering what must be the underside of the large balcony above. Hope was hardly unfamiliar with the luxury that money could buy, but even she felt as if the world had tilted on its axis the moment she had stepped through the door.

On the second floor, she found an impressive gym that stretched the entire length and width of the chalet, filled with machines that would work any muscle group imaginable, and a matted floor space just in front of the same floor-to-ceiling windows that separated it from the swimming area below. The third floor comprised of enough bedrooms for several families to share but it was the fourth floor that really impressed.

The entire open-plan floor wrapped around a chimney that hung down from the ceiling. Beneath it, a firepit blazed seductively. The floor-to-ceiling windows that had below displayed the incredible snow-covered landscape of forests and far-off chalets, here, with the elevated height offered by the fourth floor, showcased the mountain range that had become a piece of art in its own right.

Large plush cream sofas faced the central fireplace on one side, and an exquisite wooden hand-carved table ready to seat sixteen stood on the other. She became aware of a boiling kettle by the sound of it franticly rocking on its base.

Luca emerged from a doorway to her left and absently asked her if she wanted a cup of tea.

'No, Luca. I don't want a cup of tea. I want to know

why I'm here and not in the apartment I had arranged for in town,' she said, throwing her coat onto the side of the sofa.

'Because that apartment was not a secure location.'

Hope rolled her eyes, the lack of sleep as she'd worked her way through the last two days, the stress of the nomination before that—it had all worked to reduce the filter she usually kept between herself and the world.

'I'm not POTUS. Or Whitney, or any other kind of person who needs *actual* protection, Luca. Are there deeply awful and intrusive and eminently frustrating headlines about me? Yes. Do they hurt? A little bit.' A lot, actually, but she had no intention of letting him know that. 'But is my life at risk? No.'

He had patiently pulled out a cup, added a tea bag and poured the water over it throughout her little speech.

'Are you done?' he asked, without looking up.

'Excuse me?' she demanded, bristling at the inherent disrespect.

'Are you done?' he asked, turning around to face her, his hands braced behind him on the countertop and she'd have had to be blind not to see how devastatingly attractive he seemed at that moment. The black knit turtleneck jumper clung to his chest like a second skin, the matt black brushed metal of the buckle of his belt clasped tightly over his lean hips. Legs clad in dark denim, lovingly wrapping around thigh and calf muscles even the most dedicated gym fanatic would have been proud of. Lethal, deadly and downright sexy. But suddenly she became aware of the flare of his nostrils, the dragging inhalation of oxygen. He was mad. At her. Very mad.

'I don't care if you're not the President of the United States. I don't care that you're not a multi-million-dollar music industry icon. I don't care that the chunks taken out of you are done by words not weapons. That's not my business or my concern. I have been paid to do a job, and I will do that job, whether you like it or not,' Luca warned.

'I was supposed to be in town. I was supposed to be *seen* in town. *That* was the point of the distraction, Luca.'

And that just pushed him even closer to the edge. Wanting to be seen, playing with the press—she thought she was using them and couldn't see the price she was having to pay.

He stalked towards her, closing the distance between them with barely two steps.

'A job I cannot do,' he said, as if she'd not spoken, 'if *someone* in your office is leaking your every move to the press.' His words weren't shouted or yelled. They were quiet even, but hit their mark with surgical precision.

Luca saw confusion cloud that bitter chocolate gaze of hers.

'What do you mean?'

'How am I supposed to keep you safe if the press knows what you're doing before I do? The leak didn't come from my team, because *we didn't know*,' he

stressed, as infuriated by the message he'd received
from his analyst now as when he'd read the email.
'How do they know you're going to a club called
Meister? What on earth are you playing at here,
Hope?' he demanded, a red haze beginning to press
at the edges of his vision.

'I am playing the hand I've been dealt, Luca,' she
threw back, matching her heat to his. 'This is the life
I have and I'm making it work.' Fire blazed in the
molten depths now that he'd lit the fuse and he could
either stand by and watch or help her burn it all down
and, God help him, he wanted it all to burn.

'And what kind of life is that?' he demanded,
through the flames turning his vision red. 'It's vapid.
It's ridiculous,' he dismissed with a slash of his hand.
'It's all for show without any deeper meaning. You're
being used for someone else's momentary fascination
and you're allowing it. It's pathetic and beneath you
and you should know better.'

'You don't know anything about me, Luca,' she
hurled back.

And he wanted to tell her. Tell her what he knew
about her. Not just what had been in her file, not just
the facts that he'd gathered, but the smaller things he'd
noticed. The kindnesses that cost nothing but meant
everything. The concern for her staff, for the future of
her employees, for her customers. But he'd also seen
the loneliness. The hurt she hid from everyone—even
her brother. The way that she stood beneath the gaze
of those who underestimated her constantly, but still

she bore it. One day he wanted to see her rise above it, because he knew she could.

'You cannot keep me on the outside looking in,' he insisted. 'If I am constantly having to play catch-up, someone will get hurt.'

It hadn't happened yet, not on his watch, and not for any of his clients, but he couldn't take that risk, couldn't let his guard down. Not once. Not ever.

'You're doing such a good job protecting me.'

He turned his back on Hope, feeling a little too exposed, too raw. Because he'd seen it. He'd seen the moment that she'd realised he wasn't just speaking about her, about Harcourts.

'You'll tell me what you're planning?' he said, uncaring that it was more of a command than a request.

'Yes,' she said, looking at him with questions he'd put in her eyes.

He nodded and left the room.

Luca felt the loud bassline pumping out of Meister's speaker system bone-deep. It hummed beneath his skin, strangely subtle rather than jarring. He shouldn't have been surprised. He'd spent the afternoon exploring the layout, and had even done a quick walk-through before they'd opened—not that Hope would know about that.

He'd thought he'd have calmed down by now, but no. She was there, like that bassline, simmering beneath in his veins. But she was a client. Ignoring that—technically, Nate was the client—Hope was still under his protection. A client that the future success of his company rested on. A contract with Harcourts would be the first step to a global operation.

He looked around the bar area, easily spotting the press photographers who thought they were being discreet, with their camera phones pointed straight at the VIP area blocked off by two imposing security figures—one male and one female.

He wondered where his mother was right now. What she would do if she were here. She'd have been on the other side of that rope, naturally. And if she'd seen that he was here? She wouldn't have spared him a glance as she left, unwilling to risk being in the same space as the biological son she had made sign a non-disclosure agreement at the age of eighteen about their relationship. In exchange for a small inheritance, of course. She was, after all, his mother.

He willed the tension headache back from where it began to press against his temples. Hope, his mother, the press, his childhood. This was why he didn't take the lead on public image clients any more.

Hope's laughter cut through the sounds of the bar as if he'd tuned into her very essence, his awareness of her beyond professional. He clenched his teeth as he saw someone jostle her and, for the first time ever, was furious that he'd been relegated to the shadows. And while he knew that it protected them both, it grated that he was so far from his charge.

A man leaned in to whisper something in her ear. Hope smiled up at him, and he saw the gesture catch the interest of one of the paparazzi in the club. Hope cocked her head to one side, the man shifting slightly so that Luca caught a head-to-toe glimpse of her and clenched his jaw until his teeth ached.

The ruched midnight-blue satin dress which stopped at a heart-attack-inducing level on her toned thighs was enough to make a grown man weep. Although the silky material cowled around a high neck, the back was where things got dangerous. The high neck was a collar, the sleeves closing beneath the arm to keep the entirety of her back bare, announcing to the world she was braless.

From the mutinous look she'd thrown him as she'd reached for her jacket before leaving the chalet earlier that evening, he'd half believed she'd done it on purpose. Just to rile him. He hid the bitter direction of his thoughts by taking a sip of the soda that would have passed as vodka to anyone other than the barman he'd paid handsomely to ensure that Hope's drinks were un-doctored and his were non-alcoholic.

The man Hope was talking to ran a hand boldly up and down her bare arm and when she reached for him, leaning in perilously close, Luca wanted to turn away. But, grim-faced and focused, he was here to do a job, and he'd do it. So he watched from the shadows as the man pulled Hope to the dance area of the VIP section, the press in the club dropping all pretence now and simply snapping away on whatever format they could get their picture of Hope Harcourt.

As the man pulled Hope against her and Luca clenched his fists, as she let him nuzzle her neck while his hands anchored on her hips, he saw one photographer laugh, the glint of a gold tooth catching his eye and turning his stomach. Feral. Luca felt feral.

Hope spun in the man's arms, a smile across her face and, taking one of his hands, and after throwing a flirtatious wave goodbye to Angelique, she led him away from the dance floor. The man practically covered Hope with his body, blocking her from Luca's sight, and Luca stalked across the lower level, keeping them locked in his sights.

Another of the paps was already checking the pictures he'd got, a satisfied smirk pasted on his features as he probably imagined the amount of money he'd get for that shot.

Luca watched Hope open a discreet door to the back of the VIP section and disappear through it. He waited a minute, popping his jaw with a click, and left the bar.

The moment Hope got through the door to the private floors of Meister, renowned as a hook-up place for those who wanted quick, easy and discreet, she leant back against the wall, looked at Marco, the guy she'd danced with, and they both started laughing.

'Think they bought it?' Marco asked.

'Hook, line and sinker,' Hope said, returning his smile.

'Pleasure doing business with you,' replied the actor, presently trying to keep his sexuality a secret, long enough for his long-term boyfriend to prepare for the media storm that would hit the moment they went public. And they *would* go public, Hope realised, having seen the genuine love and connection the two men shared.

Envy. That was what she felt, she realised as Marco waved his goodbye and disappeared off into the car waiting for him in the underground parking garage beneath the club. But now wasn't the time for romantic hopes and dreams. Now was the time for business.

Hope made her way towards the upper floor, where a series of rooms were set out for whatever the club's clients had in mind. Meister was a sister club to the famous private members London-based club Victoriana and had been the absolutely perfect place to secretly meet with Sofia Obeid.

Hope knew the lighting was kept purposely low to ensure anyone crossing paths in the hallway would be hardly recognisable, but in the shadows she saw Luca downstairs, glaring at her. The dark promise in his gaze, desire wrapped in jealous wrapped in denial, ignited something in her. Something hot and needy. Something that had no place here, especially when she was on the brink of making a deal that would secure Harcourts' future for a *very* long time.

She reached the door of the room that she had booked for the night and knocked, aware that Sofia had arrived before Hope had left the VIP section.

'Come in,' called the voice from within.

Hope opened the door and walked in with a practised smile. She ignored the fact that she was dressed for a night of sin, in stark contrast with the sleek trouser suit worn by the other woman.

Sofia Obeid was tall and every bit as graceful as

she was elegant. Hope had done her research in the two days between the opera and when she'd made her approach through a mutual friend.

'Ms Obeid, I'm sorry for the cloak-and-dagger. I know it may seem ridiculous.'

Sofia waved aside the suggestion. 'Actually, not at all. I understand what it is like to work against family. It's not pretty and we do what we must.'

Hope nodded, noting the genuine response from the astute businesswoman. It spoke of secrets and hurts and a shared understanding forming between the two.

'Please.' Hope gestured to the seats. 'Your time is valuable and I don't want to waste it.'

'I appreciate that, thank you. I'm glad that I was in London when you reached out.'

'Rossi Industries?' Hope asked, knowing of the work Sofia had done with the property development tycoons, Alessandro and Gianni Rossi.

'Yes, the Aurora project is going well,' Sofia said with pride and excitement. 'But I must admit I'm curious as to what you might have in mind. Harcourts department stores are a global brand with instant recognition. But what that has to do with my area, I'm not yet sure.'

And Hope could understand. It wasn't immediately clear why she would reach out to a woman who owned a global chain of high-end hotels as well as numerous building development holdings.

Hope poured them each a glass of water from the side table before sitting opposite Sofia.

'You're aware that Harcourts is currently in the position of appointing a new CEO?' When Sofia nodded, Hope continued. 'My cousin Simon has a very good chance of getting that position and it would be the downfall of my family's company.'

If Sofia felt any surprise at the candour with which Hope was speaking, she hid it well. Forcing aside the insecurities she felt about assuming the position herself, Hope forged ahead. 'I would not be the shareholders' first choice and I am not naïve to that. But I know that I would do a much better job than my cousin in leading Harcourts now and into the future. To do that, I need to bring the shareholders something they can't say no to. And that's money.'

Sofia nodded and gestured for her to continue.

'Harcourts is a brand built on the promise of luxury. Harcourts can provide whatever your heart desires, as long as you have the money to pay for it and it is legal, of course. The latest fashion, the most exquisite jewellery, the most expensive furniture, the most contemporary interior design...but I want to take it a step further. I want you to be able to *live* the Harcourts lifestyle—for just a while.'

Sofia's eyes lit as she began to connect the dots. 'You want to create Harcourts hotels.'

'Yes,' Hope said, nodding fervently. 'I want to create branded luxury hotels where you can access everything that the department store has to offer, but the main focus would be on Harcourts branded items. We would start in the countries where a Harcourts department store is already located and branch out from there.'

Sofia sat up straighter in her chair. 'Okay, I get it. Makes sense, you can commute items from the store to the hotel, you already have an existing customer base in the locale on which you could expand. But where would my brand sit?'

'Harcourts Obeid.'

'Not Obeid Harcourts?'

'You already have hotels. Harcourts doesn't. Putting Harcourts first announces that it's something new.'

Hope retrieved her phone and pulled up the documents she'd put together on the deal before passing her phone to Sofia. The other woman sat back to review the proposal as Hope tried to slow her racing pulse. So much was at stake here. Her brother might have been able to lure the shareholders with Casas Fashion, but Hope not only needed something bigger, she *wanted* something bigger. Something better for Harcourts.

'I won't lie,' Sofia admitted. 'I'm tempted. Really tempted. The potential is clear, the revenue projections not only seem viable but eminently tempting. But, Hope, I can't do a deal with a marketing director.'

The other woman's words struck harder than her tone. Hope knew she didn't mean them unkindly, but simply as a statement of fact.

'If we agree to this deal, I won't *be* a marketing director, I'll be a CEO.'

Sofia shrugged. 'I've got another offer on the table.

Is it as sexy and exciting as this? No. Would I rather work with you? Absolutely. But you know that this will be a problem with anyone you take this offer to.'

Hope clenched her teeth, her worst fears confirmed. She knew Sofia was right, but she also knew how good her idea was.

'Tell me why you want this,' Sofia stated.

Hope's mind went blank for a heartbeat. 'For the good of Harcourts. It will secure my family company's position as a leading global brand and bring both our companies huge revenue.'

For the first time in their conversation, Sofia seemed a little disappointed. It was there and gone in the blink of an eye but, whatever it had been, Hope realised *that* was the moment she lost Sofia Obeid.

'Can you give me some time? Think on it? Please,' Hope asked, hating that she would beg, hating the desperation she felt clawing at her.

'I'm returning to London in an hour.'

Hope felt sick.

'I could be back here in two days,' Sofia offered.

Hope wasn't sure if it was a lifeline or pity, but she took it with both hands.

'Absolutely. You let me know when and I'll make it happen,' Hope said automatically as she tried to catalogue how badly the outcome of this meeting had affected her.

Luca leant against the wall in the seating area of the private floor above Meister, ignoring the plush leather sofas and chairs. The urge to pace like a caged animal was a need in his blood. He didn't like knowing that he couldn't see what was going on in the room.

It didn't matter that Hope was in there with a business associate—which was all she'd told him earlier as they'd made the plans for that evening. He wasn't sure which had annoyed him more, that she refused to trust him or the thought of her in there with another man.

But something had happened to him, watching Hope on that dance floor. Something that had turned him from cool, calm and in control to raging neanderthal. He'd been attracted to women before. He'd chased and been chased, but the sheer indifference that Hope hid behind—because he knew she was hiding her desire, just like he was—drove him to the brink in a way he hadn't known before.

A door in the hallway opened and a tall, elegant woman emerged. Head down and turning away from Luca, she disappeared towards the back exit of the club. He barely gave her a second glance before he was at the threshold of the room he knew Hope was in.

He waited in the open doorway, unwilling to enter the room, desperately needing to keep some space between them. It was the first time he didn't trust himself. The first time ever. But as he looked to where Hope sat, staring into the distance, he realised that the meeting hadn't gone well.

'We can't go back to London yet,' she said, staring at the wall.

'Okay.'

'We'll be here for another two days, maybe three.'

'What happened?' he asked, wanting to know so that he could fix it, so that he could take that look from her face.

She shook her head as if unable to put words to it.

'She said no?' he demanded.

She looked up at him as if seeing him for the first time. 'She won't sign unless I'm CEO.'

'But you won't be CEO if she doesn't sign,' he said, realising the predicament instantly. 'What did she actually say?'

'She wanted to know why I want to do the deal. And then that we should both think about it.'

He frowned, wondering how Hope had answered the question, wondering what would have swayed the woman who had just left the room by a discreet back exit.

'You'll make it happen,' he said confidently but absently, distracted by the hemline of her dress, which had ridden up on her thighs. She had turned him into an animal.

'Why?' she asked, genuine curiosity in her eyes. 'Why do you think that?'

'Because that's what you do,' he answered as if it were the most obvious thing in the world. 'People underestimate you and you prove them wrong.'

There was an imperceptible breath held between them. He'd been too observant. He'd betrayed himself in an instant. He knew it. She knew it.

Hope stood and closed the distance between them and he held his ground, refusing to back away from what had become nearly the greatest threat he'd ever experienced.

'Why are you angry?' she demanded.

'It doesn't matter,' he dismissed quickly. Too quickly.

'Yes, it does. Why are you angry with me?'

He felt it burning in his gaze. The frustration, the helpless fury, the indignation and the want. It was all too much.

'You let that man put his hands on you,' he growled.

CHAPTER SEVEN

HOPE BACKED UP as he stepped towards her, crossing over the threshold, closing the door behind him and coming into the room. Not because she was scared but because she didn't know what to do with all that testosterone.

'You let that man touch you,' he said, rephrasing his objection to what had happened in the VIP section of Meister, closing the distance between them so that his chest pressed up against hers.

And a purely feminine power unfurled deep within her, knowing that she'd made him jealous. That he wanted her enough to be jealous. Standing in the centre of the room, she knew there was plenty she could do to create space between them if she needed to. If she *wanted* to. But she didn't. She was tired of running from this, running from how she felt about this man, from how much she wanted this man. And instead she breathed deeply, the action pressing her chest against his with the force of her inhalation, causing fireworks to ignite in his silvery gaze.

Tonight, he was dressed in a dark grey shirt, a thin

black tie hanging down the centre of his broad chest.
His shirtsleeves were rolled back and he looked like
he belonged in the shadows. What she wanted to do
felt like it belonged in the shadows.

He peered down at her, his height requiring her to
crane her neck just a bit, just enough.

'Yes, I let him touch me,' Hope said into the thick
tension weaving between them. Taunting him was
dangerous—instinctively, she knew that, but she also
craved it.

A part of Hope registered that this was crazy. She
didn't do things like this. Having been burned by too
many people posing as her friends only for access to
what they could sell to the nearest journalist, she was
incredibly careful about who she spent time with.

But this was entirely different. *He* was different.
She knew that as well as she knew her own name. It
was in his clear distaste for the media, in his intense
discomfort with anything to do with them, in the
anger she'd seen barely restrained at the headlines
he believed her cousin to be involved in. But whatever this was—her feelings for him—she didn't have
control over it. It was as if she was being swept away
by it and there was something inherently seductive
about that. About letting go. About just letting go.

'Did he ask?'

'What?' she said, his question cutting through the
fog of desire clouding her mind.

'Did he ask before he put his hands on you?'

Dark, swirling, thick and heavy, promises filled
his gaze and she almost didn't answer.

'Yes. He did.'

'And if I asked?'

This time his chest heaved in a breath that she felt against her breasts, hardness pressing into nipples that were taut with need.

She could play dumb, she could pretend she didn't understand what he meant, but then she would have to walk away. She felt it. They stood there on the cusp, the brink of an edge she could still step back from. But she didn't want to.

'What would it mean if I said yes?' she asked, and for a second she thought he might tease her. Laugh at her, ask if she was demanding hearts and roses and promises she wasn't sure she wanted herself. Fear made her look straight ahead, staring at his chest and feeling the anticipated embarrassment beginning to burn her cheeks.

Her heart pounded in her chest as she waited for him to answer and, even though a second stretched into ten, she refused to raise her gaze. Finally, his thumb hooked beneath her chin and she lifted her head to look deep into his silvery gaze.

Dark tousled hair framed his face perfectly and she was instantly struck by how beautiful he truly was. Fine cheekbones balanced out the sharp angles of his face, but it was him—it was his power beneath the layers of skin and silver eyes, that made him so devastating.

'If you asked me to put my hands on you, it would mean that we would be adults about this. It would mean that when we get back to London, you'll have someone else who will look out for you. I'll oversee it, but I won't be involved in your close protection detail.'

'And what about my brother?'

'You want to talk about your brother right now?' he demanded, the gentle tease so much more welcome than what she'd feared only moments ago.

'What about the deal? He wanted you personally to—'

'He'll live with it,' Luca said, shifting his weight between his feet, somehow making her feel as if he wanted to walk her back a step, even though he hadn't moved.

'But—'

'He'll live with it,' Luca growled, and she got the distinct impression he was barely holding on.

'So if I *did* ask you to put your hands on me?' she asked, needing to know. Needing clarification before they both gave in to whatever madness was waiting to take over.

That she was even considering this was insanity. But perhaps it was because they both had so much to lose that she was willing to take the risk. He had the future of his company on the line as much as she had the future of hers.

'It would mean,' he said, his head dropping closer to hers, his breath puffs of air against her moistened lips, 'that I get to put my hands on you whenever I want, until we return.'

'Just until we return...' She didn't even know if she were asking or demanding and from the swirling in the grey of his eyes like molten silver, neither did he. She was almost dizzy with want, but her instincts kicked in just in time. 'In private,' she said.

'What?' he asked, as if struggling with the same heady sensuality.

'This is only in private.'

Something dark passed across his features, so quickly she wasn't sure that she'd seen it, but then she was half lost because he said, 'Of course.'

'I can't—' Something in her started to defend herself. The risks she couldn't take—the risks neither of them could.

'I get it. So, in private,' he said, pulling his hands from his pockets, where he'd fisted them, 'I get to put my hands on you whenever I want?' They were there, hanging seemingly loose, despite the tension she felt coursing through every inch of his body, inches from where she wanted them.

'Yes.' The word was sin on her lips.

'Say it,' he commanded.

'I want your hands on my body.'

The words were magic for Luca, making the iron-strong bonds of his restraint disappear in an instant. He'd wanted this woman from the first moment he'd laid eyes on her and he could have lied, told himself he didn't know where he wanted to start, but he didn't have time for that. He knew exactly where he wanted his hands.

He pressed the length of his body against hers, crowding her, thrilled when she didn't back up and give him space. He felt a wicked smile pull at the curve of his lips as his knuckles grazed the hemline of Hope's skirt, pulled tight across her thighs.

He flexed his thumb and brushed across the satin of her skin just beneath the skirt of her dress, sending a scattering of goosebumps across her thighs. He could tell that she was trying to hide her reaction to him, unsure whether it was a hangover from the days they'd spent fighting their attraction or whether she was making him work for it, and both turned him on just as much.

He slipped his hand between her thighs and gently pressed her legs apart just an inch or two. He watched her face like a hawk—the way her lips parted just enough to suck a shocked inhale through them, the way her brown eyes burned with even just the hint of heat between them. Her chest was still pressed against his, but he could see the pulse flickering at her neck and he wanted to cover it with his open mouth, to feel that beat on his tongue.

Wicked. What he wanted to do with her was wicked. The heat from her legs warmed his hand as he palmed both thighs, sweeping round to run his thumb across the curve of her arse. A gentle roll unfurled through her body as she grew slightly longer in her spine when the back of his hand met the damp material of her panties.

He held back from doing what he wanted, which was to walk her back to the bare wall behind her and devour her. While that would be delicious and something he would absolutely do before returning to London, tonight was about Hope—her needs and her wants.

He caressed her thighs gently, again and again, almost accidentally brushing against her core as it grew damper and hotter each time. He felt her urge to move, to take control, to seek the pleasure he was denying her, but she didn't—and he knew how much that must cost her. Because it was driving him out of his mind. Every inch of his body was sensitised and tuned to her frequency, to her.

She opened her mouth, the plea in her eyes before it made it to her lips.

'Don't,' he commanded. 'Don't beg—you don't ever beg with me. Just ask. Ask for what you want,' he said, not missing a moment of how she felt about what he'd just said. Relief, thanks, excitement, arousal. And it infuriated him that someone had taught her that she couldn't just ask. As if she didn't have the right to pleasure on her own terms. He forced down the anger and twisted it into something else, something deliciously sinful.

'Oh, Hope. I'm going to give you so much pleasure you're not going to be the same again,' he promised.

The taunt, the promise, the cocky arrogance he knew she would rise to meet, worked.

'Really? You talk a good game, Luca, but—'

Her words slipped into a gasp as he ran his thumb between the folds outlined by the damp silk of her panties. She shivered beneath his touch as his caress became more purposeful and less playful.

Hope's head fell back, the long line of her neck exposed and, unable to resist, he bent forward to press his lips against her skin. Open-mouthed, he gorged on the salty sweetness of her. Her murmur became a purr of pleasure as his fingers slipped past the wet silk to tease her and finally, *finally*, he had what he wanted. Hope—hot, wet and wanting in his arms.

Impatience choked him, clogging his throat with a desire so thick he could barely breathe past it. His pulse pounded in his veins and his ears like a drum, an incessant refrain. Taste, taste, taste.

He hooked a thumb around the thin band of her panties. 'May I?' he asked, his voice gravel against the satin of her throat.

'Yes… Luca?' she asked, her head straightening, waiting until he pulled away from her neck and looked her in the eye.

'Give it to me. All of it. All the pleasure you promised. I don't want to ask again.'

Oh, she was incredible, this woman.

There, in her eyes, he saw the heat that matched his own, saw the need, the desire, the passion and the power. He didn't have to hold back with her and she didn't have to pretend to be less with him.

In response, he sank to his knees. Not quickly but slowly, so she could see, so she could imagine what he was going to do to her. Like this, he was level with the juncture of her thighs, and he didn't think he'd ever find anywhere else he'd want to be more.

One hand pushed up the ruched side of the dress as the other pulled her panties down, a delicious tension between the two opposing forces, revealing a delicate crosshatch of curls. Musk on the air and heat from her body so close he could practically taste it turned his own arousal from painful to near unbearable. His erection pressed hard against the zip of his trousers, but he ignored it over a much more pressing need.

He ran his thumb between her folds again, one hand behind her, supporting her as she shivered in response, the tremble of her legs a victory, the gasp of heady need his rallying cry and the taste of her as he spread her for him, as he pressed the most intimate of kisses to her core, the only reward he would ever need.

Hope was shivering between fire and ice. Her lungs sucking in oxygen like she was drowning, because that was what he was doing to her. Drowning her in pleasure, just like he'd promised.

Sex—and it had only been sex—with Martin, had been perfunctory. Bed based, missionary, near mathematical, calculated. As if it were something he was assessing himself on. But this? This was sensuality, this was exquisite, powerful, *arcane*. This was what femininity was. This was what adoration was, she thought, before Luca fastened his attention and his teeth gently on her clitoris.

She bit her lip to stop the groan of pleasure that begged for release.

'I want to hear you,' he said against her core, before laving her with his tongue in a way that nearly had her coming right then.

She wasn't sure she could do it. She wasn't sure

that, after years of not, owning her pleasure vocally was something she could…and then she didn't have a choice. Luca didn't give her one. He teased his fingers into her slowly but surely, at the same time grinding his tongue against her clitoris, bringing her to the brink of mindlessness, where she had absolutely no control over the pants of need falling from her mouth.

Pushed by his relentless pursuit of her pleasure, closer and closer to stand before the impending orgasm that felt bigger than anything she'd experienced before, she tried to hide from it, but Luca wouldn't let her. He made her acknowledge the force of it, welcome it, bear it as it crashed down about her. Wave after wave collapsed over her as she sobbed for breath, for mercy, for more, she didn't know any more.

By the time she came back to herself, Luca stood from where he had knelt before her and was pressing open-mouthed kisses to her neck. His hands gently caressed her sensitised skin, warming her body to his all over again. Her pulse had barely settled into a satiated throb when his thumb found her taut nipple and he pressed his tongue over the material it strained against.

There were too many barriers between them. Too many layers. She wanted to feel him, to know the heat of his skin, the firm muscle beneath his shirt and the erection pressing against her abdomen—the weight of it, the velvety smoothness, the *taste* of it. Carnal and wicked images ran through her mind like a kaleidoscope and suddenly she was ravenous for whatever he could give her, whatever he would let her take.

Luca's hands bracketed her ribs, holding her to his mouth…to where he continued to fasten his mouth to her breast. The cowl neckline of her dress was too high for him to bare her to his tongue without damaging it or… Frustration and impatience had her reaching for the bottom of her dress and pulling it from her body, Luca reacting quickly enough to move out of the way to let her. And then she stood before him, her black heels with the red soles, and absolutely nothing else.

And that was when Hope truly understood what it was to be devoured. He consumed every inch of her. She followed his gaze as his eyes tracked over her breasts, lingering on them before following the curve of her hip, the length of her legs, the sweep of her calves, locking on the shoes, when she saw silver *burn*.

'Turn,' he commanded.

If it had been anyone else, she might have felt objectified, but with Luca? She felt *alive*. She felt desired. She felt as if she were the one with the power and he was simply asking for more. Slowly, inch by inch, she turned in a circle, feeling the heat of his attention like a touch, like a caress, warmed by it, wetted by it.

Restless, she rubbed her thighs together, knowing that the orgasm he'd brought her to was a taste of what was to come, rather than the culmination. He bit his lip as he tugged at his tie and shirt with staccato movements. Buttons were yanked, his belt released from loops in one smooth movement that defied rational thought, his feet were bare and she couldn't remember when he'd taken off his shoes.

He pulled his shirt from his body, the vest beneath hugging muscles she wanted easy access to. Refusing to be a spectator any longer, she closed the distance between them and tugged the vest from the waistband of his trousers, glorying in the hot, smooth muscles that rippled beneath her touch.

She traced the detail of his tattoo, the wing down to the body of the horse. Pegasus. Power, freedom, determination all communicated in black and white detail—it was a piece of art.

He let her explore his body with a patience that she marvelled at. It was only when she pulled the vest from his body, pressing her mouth against his, her head full of the scent of him, her tongue parsing salt from skin and the taste that was uniquely him, that she realised it wasn't patience, it was restraint. And it was fraying beneath her ministrations.

Satisfaction unfurled and her own impatience got the better of her. She pulled him to her by the waistband of his trousers, before reaching to undo the button and the zip. Matching his earlier sensual tease, she allowed the back of her hand to smooth down the long length of his powerful erection. The temptation of it, of what she would feel when he filled her, was too much. She turned her hand to grasp him, her hold firm but gentle, the thin cotton of his briefs doing nothing to disguise the promise of him, and even that barrier became too much. She wanted skin, she wanted… Her hand slipped beneath his briefs and held him, heat on heat, smooth on smooth, but, even then, less than they both wanted.

Her hand drew up and down the length of him, the slide erotic and bringing slashes of dark red to his cheekbones. His chest heaved with his breath, and she felt it, having him at her mercy, the power she wielded in that moment. The trust it had taken for her to give in to him shining back at her in his silvery gaze. His breaths became pants and groans as she flexed her grip at the base of his erection, as she reached to cup his balls, as he fought his own desire for more.

It wasn't enough. She wanted him inside her. As if he'd read her very thoughts, he pulled back slightly from her hold, breaking their connection, only to remove the trousers and briefs in one go. If she had even a moment to take in what they looked like, staring each other down, naked, aroused, panting, it was just that. A moment. Because Luca reached for her, picking her up in his arms, her legs instinctively wrapping around his waist, his erection pressing against her stomach, his hands beneath her, perilously close to her folds, teasing her and instantly making her throb. He held her as he walked back to the sofa and sat, laying her across his lap, looking up hungrily at where she rose above him.

Unable to stop herself, she ground against his erection, the pressure raking against her clitoris sending a thrill through her, and his hands on her backside only encouraging her to repeat the action.

He reached down beside them and returned with a condom and she sent a prayer of thanks that at least one of them was thinking sensibly. She rose onto her knees as he covered himself in the latex, before running his thumb between her folds again, teasing her clitoris from beneath her. Unrestrained moans of pleasure fell from her lips as she rocked against his thumb, as he guided the head of his penis to her entrance and then she slowly, inch by inch, sank downwards onto his erection.

Curses fell into the room, his or hers she couldn't tell as he filled her, stretching her aching muscles, pleasure feeding into her bloodstream like a drug she could become addicted to. From this position she had power, she had control, and that he knew her enough to know how important that was to her was both terrifying and thrilling. Back and forth she rocked against him, teasing them both, sweat slicking their bodies and heartbeats pounding through skin.

For what felt like hours, they simply gloried in the feel of each other, the sounds and feel and scent and taste of each other... It was languid, slow and utterly erotic, the slide and glide of his hard length in her. The pleasure merely banked from her previous orgasm nipped at her heels, building slowly and slowly, and all the while Luca's gaze locked on hers watched every single moment of it happen. He could feel it, she realised, the tightening of her muscles, the impending orgasm about to sweep her away.

But then he moved.

Luca reached around her back, his palms on the tops of her shoulders, and pulled her down at the same moment as he pushed upward and the earth tilted on its axis. He was so deep in her he felt lost and found at the same time. Again and again, he thrust, hard and deep and quick. His hold kept them joined, but each time he felt closer and closer to impossible. Sweat gathered at the base of his spine, Hope, slippery in his arms, her pleasure-filled cries burnt into his soul as he shoved them closer and closer to the brink he wasn't sure he wanted to cross.

More, he *needed* more.

He picked her up and held her to him as he changed their positions, laying Hope carefully on her back on the sofa, and nearly losing his breath as he parted her thighs, so that he could see the way his erection penetrated her body, that he impaled her, but it was Hope watching him that pushed him towards the cliff edge. Her pleasure in his pleasure, her arousal fed by his, and he reached between them, his thumb finding her clitoris, rubbing gently, furiously, wringing cries and pleas from a woman who had struggled to find her voice merely an hour before.

'Luca,' she cried, his name pulled from a voice stretched taut with desire. His chest felt thick, full with arousal, barely able to breathe as he shoved into her, deep and hard, pulling out only to shove into her again. Braced on a hand beside her head, he pounded again and again, pushing them to madness.

Her hands wrapped around his forearm, her mouth finding his wrist, biting, licking and hiding her desire, her skin flushed and sweat-slick as her moans reached a crescendo, the muscles wrapped around his erection tightening like a fist and the orgasm that struck them both at the same time pulled them into an abyss of two stars exploding together.

Hope couldn't stop staring at him. This man, who had given her the most sensual, erotic experience of her life. This man, who had promised to touch her whenever he wanted, in private. And, as clichéd as it sounded, she was changed by what they had just shared. She felt it, it had sunk into her bones. A secret knowing of what she was capable of not only giving but receiving. As if she'd accessed some previously unknown, untapped, potential for *more*.

Luca navigated the car effortlessly through the snow-covered darkness. A silence that should have been suffocating, stifling even, held nothing but satisfaction. But also curiosity, she realised as she watched him palm the wheel, turning into the near invisible road to their chalet.

Is it always like that? For you? she wondered.

It was only when he turned to look at her, the car slowly pulling to a stop, heat blazing in his steel-grey gaze that she realised she'd spoken out loud.

'No, Hope. It's never…' He trailed off, seemingly as incapable of describing what they'd shared as she was, soothing the thin thread of unease that had un- wound within her. It was important to her that they were equally in this, whatever this was, until they returned to London. Two days. She had two days to work Luca out of her system—if that was even possible. And two days to figure out how to convince Sofia Obeid to change her mind.

He leaned his head back against the rest and looked at her. 'Stop thinking so hard,' he said. 'It's late. And I still have things I want to do to you tonight.'

And on that sensual promise, Hope let herself be led from the car, into the bedroom, where Luca once again drowned her in a pleasure she could have barely imagined before that night.

CHAPTER EIGHT

HOPE WOKE WITH a stretch. The bed was obscenely comfortable, the snowscape through the windows a skier's fantasy. Her body ached pleasantly and her blood was still heavy with the drug that was Luca. She nestled into the pillow that still bore his scent and warmth. She squinted at the clock on the side table and rolled onto her back with a groan.

It was seven a.m. and, no matter where she was in the world, she never slept in this late. She should have been in the gym, showered, dressed and on her way to work by now. And even though she was in Austria, despite last night's diversions, she *was* here to work.

She slipped from beneath the covers and peered into the en suite bathroom. The shower stall took up half the wall and she approved. Hugely. With a smile, she worked out the buttons and within seconds was standing under a powerfully hot stream of water, bringing her mentally into the present.

Less than fifteen minutes later, she emerged onto the fourth-floor living area dressed in soft, easy yoga clothes and looking for Luca. She found him leaning back against the counter, looking out at the forest at the foot of the mountains and the smooth slopes that brought visitors here in their thousands.

She paused, her hand on her stomach, taking in the sight. He stood there bare-chested, black silk pants hanging low on his hips, almost as if their sole purpose was to display the corded muscles that veed beneath the waistband. She knew what those corded muscles could do, she realised, the blush riding high on her cheeks. She should be hitting the brakes on whatever this was. It wouldn't, *couldn't*, last. But a selfish part of her wanted more. Wanted to luxuriate in it, *him*, just a little longer.

He looked at her then, catching her watching him. 'Morning,' he said, his voice gravelly, in the same tone he'd used last night to tell her all the things he wanted to do to her and more.

All she was capable of was nodding. He held out a mug of steaming coffee and the spell was lifted and she covered the distance between them, desperate to get at her *other* morning addiction. She was sure that things would make sense after even just half a cup. And if they didn't, then she would make them make sense.

She went to stand beside him and paused when she caught sight of his tablet, open on the website for the *London Daily*. There was a headline about a politician lying about his expenses next to a photograph of her and Marco dancing in the club.

Unable to stop herself, she reached for the tablet, clicking on the post.

Hope Harcourt Drowns Sorrows with Stranger!

'I don't think Marco would appreciate being called a stranger,' she commented, scanning the hastily written hack piece on her 'indiscreet night' following hot on the heels of her ex-fiancé's new engagement. At least there was no mention of Sofia. 'It worked,' she observed, intensely uncomfortable searching the headlines of other magazines and articles for news of her supposed scandalous affair, standing beside the man she *had* actually spent the night with.

She knew the cover story was needed—if Simon had even an inkling of what she was up to, he'd find a way either to ruin it or try to trump her. No, it was best if he and the board all thought she was sunning herself on a ski slope until she could execute her plan—*if* she could execute her plan. But it left a bitter taste in her mouth to use herself in such a way.

And that was exactly what she felt like. *Used.* Dirty in a way no man had ever made her feel before. And for once, just once, she wanted to have a day where she wasn't in the spotlight, where she wasn't fodder for another attack by either the newspapers or Harcourts.

'You're thinking too much again,' he growled as he watched her take her first sip, testing the heat, testing the strength. Of the coffee and the man, she thought, perhaps.

'I can't *not* think, Luca. Everything rests on this deal with Obeid,' she said, shaking her head, feeling that sense of helplessness again. 'If Simon gets his way, I won't be able to just sit there and watch him ruin the company my father…' She trailed off, unable to admit how much she needed this to work. For her father, her brother, her grandfather. She tried to ignore the way that Luca narrowed his eyes at her. 'I'm going to use the gym…'

She trailed off at the way Luca was slowly shaking his head and felt a flare of frustration. Being dominant in the bedroom was one thing, but if he thought for one minute that extended out of it, into her day-to-day life, then—

'We're going skiing,' he announced.

'I have work,' she said, her hackles rising.

'You know your work. You know that deal. You know what wiggle room you have, and so does Sofia Obeid. What you need to do is work out what she wants. Because she does want this deal, or she would have given you a flat *no*.'

The reason in his tone was as infuriating as the fact that he was right. She *did* need to get out of her head. Hope looked past him to the golden rays of the early morning sun glistening on fresh snow. He was the devil, tempting her in more ways than one.

Luca was almost surprised that Hope had agreed. It hadn't actually been what he'd intended to say, or even how he'd intended they spent the day. But the shadows in her gaze hadn't been from a lack of sleep, even if there had been very few moments stolen in between the times they'd reached for each other through the night.

He'd meant what he'd said. It had never been like

that for him and he wasn't sure what that meant, and he didn't want to try to find that out just yet either. He got the impression that Hope felt the same way.

Luca turned to find Hope making her way towards him, her ski boots crunching on the snow. Even wrapped up in insulated layers of ski gear, she was stunning. Most of her blonde hair was hidden by the helmet, aside from the few wisps that had escaped. Goggles hung around her neck and her cheeks had a healthy pink glow from a mixture of excitement and windchill.

Unlike him, dressed head to toe in uniform black, she'd found ski pants in a deep orange and a high-tech slender pale blue jacket. Obviously the latest fashion, but he knew the brand, knew its quality was of the highest degree. He wondered if she would ever not stand out in a crowd. It was just something about her. Something he wasn't sure she realised she had.

'There's a path through the forest that leads straight down to the bottom of the slopes. From there we can get the chairlift up and take one of the green runs over to the other side of the range, where the slopes are a little more challenging, if you like.'

She appraised him. 'You ski regularly?'

'When I can,' he replied. Alma and Pietro hadn't had any interest in the sport, but the school his mother had paid for had regularly arranged trips to slopes in Italy and across Europe. The innate grace he'd inherited from Anna meant that he was a natural, and he'd enjoyed the athleticism of it as much as the beauty of where skiing could take him. He'd loved every minute, until the coach journey home. Because he'd known then that it was only hours before he'd watch each and every one of his friends rush off the coach, eager to get to their parents, to tell them about their holiday, to get kisses and be enveloped in hugs. And he'd wait, making sure to be the last off the coach, so that there were fewer people who might see Pietro, standing beside his old car, grim-faced and unwelcoming.

Anna had never seen it or, if she had, she'd refused to acknowledge it, but Pietro and Alma had only ever wanted to please the famous actress. Anna had been such a bright, shining light to them that they would have done anything she'd asked of them. Even raise her child. But it had never meant anything more to them than a burden they bore for her.

Hope clipped her boots into the skis provided by the chalet, their boot and ski measurements provided in the booking so that the guests wouldn't need to go through the rigmarole of battling against the general population renting their equipment. Luca bent to check them for himself, ignoring the smirk pulling her full lips into a curve. Satisfied she was ready, he clipped back into his and pushed off along the private path that led through the forest.

The sound of the skis on snow, the *thunk* of the poles digging into the ground was soothing on nerves almost painfully and constantly aware of Hope. There was something almost magical about it: the seclusion of the trees, their rich, vivid emerald peeking beneath thick layers of white, the way that sound was dull and that the easy movement caused his pulse to raise gently. He felt Hope keeping pace with him and smiled, wondering how long that would last.

They emerged from the forest near to the chairlift that would take them up higher, where they could take a series of runs that would get them to where he wanted to take Hope. She pulled to a stop beside him, pulling her goggles down, her eyes bright with excitement and expectation, and he knew he'd done the right thing.

'Your chariot awaits,' he said, pointing to the bottom of the chairlift, surrounded by small groups of families, couples and what looked like a ski class of five-year-olds.

Anonymity. He'd given her anonymity, she realised, as she leaned into the gentle turn she took down the green run that both she and Luca could have made blindfold. But she enjoyed the ease of it, refamiliarising herself with the turns, the stops, the feel of it. She'd spent so long being the face of Harcourts, courting the press, for good or ill, because it was how she represented her family, that she'd forgotten about simple pleasures, of an enjoyment that wasn't on display—perhaps even of a romance that was secret, she thought, her stomach swooping in line with the wide arc she made with her skis as she turned to a stop at the bottom of another set of lifts. To one side was the button lift, dragging skiers up the side of the easy run full of children and newbies. To the other was the bubble lift and where Luca was leading her to.

They queued up with excited children and eager adults, all speaking a mix of German, French, English, Spanish and Italian. Hope felt happy. And excited. A family of four stepped into the bubble-shaped lift behind them, the heavy plastic affording a hazy glimpse of the slopes below them and the mountain range above. The little girl was jumping up and down, the thrill and excitement rolling off her in waves. But it was the little boy that caught Hope's eye. Solemn, perhaps a little scared, his mother quietly and gently soothed him with reassuring words Hope didn't need to understand.

She remembered her mother doing something very similar for her when she and Nate had been learning to ski. She caught Luca looking at them too and wondered what it reminded him of. And slowly the smile that had curved her lips dropped a little. The look in his gaze wasn't one of fond memories.

But the lift arrived at its destination and they only had a short time to grab their skis and disembark. She went to follow the family to the top of the blue run—a step up in difficulty from the green, but Luca gently guided her in the opposite direction.

'We're not taking the run down?' she asked.

'Not yet. There's something I want to show you,' he said. 'Trust me?' And even though she couldn't see his eyes, hidden by the wraparound sunglasses, there was a taunt, a challenge, without the edge and with all the tease that she enjoyed so much between them.

'Not as far as I can throw you,' she lied and Luca

threw his head back and laughed. It was a startling sound—one that drew more than just her glance his way.

'Come on,' he said, and he guided her towards a faint track. It was off-piste, so it wasn't under careful management, and there were no ski patrols keeping an eye out like there were on the runs. But Hope was confident of both her and Luca's ability and she knew he'd never put her at risk. Ever.

The thought was as startling as his sudden deep laugh had been and it rang in her ears, echoing in the silence created by the banks of snow that surrounded them as they crossed the ridge of the hill and swept down into the basin below.

Her stomach rose and fell as the momentum they'd created forced them back up the other side and, despite her absolute conviction that she would slide back down, she found herself cresting the other side and couldn't help but let out a whoop of pleasure.

She followed Luca as he cut a path across fresh, untouched snow, and she tried not to be distracted by the sight of clouds hovering close by. He called back to her to make sure she was keeping up and while the cold air pushed and pulled out of her lungs with a frequency that was as intense as any workout, it was so much more satisfying.

For a while she focused simply on that. Moving her body, following Luca's direction. Her mind emptied for the first time in what felt like for ever. Peaceful. It was peaceful. There was nothing here that wanted her to be, or do, something. There were no demands on her or for her to make. She settled into the rhythm and lost herself, until Luca slowed to a stop. There was a little wooden sign, but she missed what it said because the moment she gazed to where Luca was looking, she forgot her curiosity.

Breath left her chest in a whoosh, the sight before her so magnificent. The peak of a mountain rose up so close she was half convinced she could reach out to touch it. The clouds that had hovered near earlier ringed the peak below where they stood.

When Luca clicked out of his skis and took a seat in the small bank of snow behind them, Hope followed suit.

'It's beautiful,' she said, her tone reverent. It was as if they were close to heaven, she thought, the sun glinting off the snow, a pale denim blue sky bare from but a few spun-sugar clouds. It was spectacular.

Luca nodded, not needing to fill the silence between them. It was an unusual trait, she realised, suddenly aware of how much of her life was filled with distractions or information. She had wondered before if it were part of his role, his job. A chauffeur needed to be unassuming and invisible a lot of the time. In some ways, she supposed, bodyguards had to be the same. But she was beginning to realise that it was something innate in him. Something quiet that called to the near frantic energy of her life and drew it down a few notches, soothing her in a way she'd not experienced before.

Her grandfather tolerated her, challenged her to be better and more with his absent manner and his criticism. Nate sought to fix, to mend, to do, unaware that he was utterly overcrowding her, not even giving her the chance to prove herself. The board, the shareholders, they were simply blind to what she achieved daily. But Luca? He just let her be.

Luca felt the moment that she relaxed finally. For the first time since that morning, she took the breath he'd felt her struggling for. He knew the breakneck speed at which she worked; he knew enough about the life she led to understand why she felt the need to be that way. He just wasn't sure that she'd ever really sat down and thought about whether she wanted it or not.

It hadn't been Alma or Pietro, or even Anna, that had helped him to see what he wanted from life, but a teacher from his local school in Palizzi. Signor Arcuri had called him back after class, just before the end of his final term.

'It doesn't matter what you want to do, Luca. As long as you know why. That "why" will give you purpose. It will see you through hard times, self-doubt, poverty and riches alike. Find why you want to do what it is you want to do, and do it with absolute conviction and no looking back.'

It had changed his life, Luca knew. It had forced him to coalesce his thoughts, his wants, into a single goal: Pegaso.

Perhaps he'd never grown out of the idea of becoming the white knight he'd believed his mother had desperately needed, because even then he'd known that he wanted to protect people. To help those who couldn't help themselves. So he'd taken the money his mother had gifted him when he'd signed the NDA at eighteen and been clever. Sensible but clever. He'd invested half of that money while he'd done the training and groundwork needed to build Pegaso up from nothing. He was proud of that, and he'd never looked back. But he couldn't help but wonder if that perhaps all this action and forward momentum in Hope disguised the fact that she didn't know what it was that she truly wanted.

'Beats the gym,' Hope said, her breath a puff of air, her eyes squinting in the sun, having taken off her goggles to look at the view.

'Beats the gym,' he confirmed. He checked his watch. 'Come on.'

'Have we got somewhere to be?' she asked, laughing lightly. It was a sound he felt against his skin. One he wanted more of.

'A very important meeting,' he teased.

Another ninety minutes of skiing and one chairlift later and they came to a large chalet, similar to the one they were staying in, but here on the large wraparound deck were tables, half full of skiers and families. Hope's desire for anonymity was so different to his mother's near compulsive need for recognition that he didn't know how to make it fit with Hope and her life.

'Lunch?' she asked, turning that bright, full smile on him, and it had the force of a punch to the chest, sending all thoughts of his mother scattering.

'Best place in town,' he commented.

'It's the *only* place in town,' she observed, making a show of looking around at the miles of snow-covered landscape.

'Doesn't mean that it's not good,' he said, holding his hand out to her. When she took it, he led her up the busy wooden steps and towards the entrance.

Stop.

It was a feeling. The raising of hairs on his neck. He'd never not trusted it because it had always been right. He stopped and turned. Something had caught his eye; he just couldn't quite work out...

There.

The man had his back half-turned now, but Luca could just make out the high-quality camera. And yes, it could have been a skier using personal equipment, but there was something about him that was familiar.

The club. He'd seen the guy at the club. Luca remembered him because of his tooth, having tried to work out if it was a stain or a gold replacement that had caught his eye when the guy smiled.

Before he could think it through, Luca covered the distance between them and crowded in on the man, using their height difference to maximum effect. The photographer turned, ready to lash out, but shrank back instead when he realised it was Luca.

'Give me the camera,' Luca said, his voice low but determined.

'Hey, man, I'm just doing my—'

'Not today,' Luca said, reaching for the camera.

'You can't do that,' the photographer complained.

'I can delete the ones from just now, or I can take the SD card. Your choice.'

'How magnanimous of you,' the pap whined.

'Card it is,' Luca said, flipping the camera, pressing the button.

'No, wait—wait. That's my work.'

'And this is mine,' Luca said, a penetrating glare forcing the photographer's eyes away.

'Just the ones from now,' he said, his tone placating but his eyes furious. 'Please.'

Luca probably should have taken the SD card, but he knew he was skating on thin ice. With no justification for removing the pictures, other than the fact that he had wanted to give her, give them, this one day, he scanned through them. The clearest one showed Hope—and it clearly was Hope Harcourt—looking up at him and taking his hand. He paused for a heartbeat before hitting the delete button on the pictures.

Luca thrust the camera back at the photographer and stalked back to Hope, who stood waiting nervously, casting furtive glances over his shoulder at the man behind him.

'How did he find us?' she whispered.

'I don't know, but he has nothing now.'

'You deleted the images?'

He looked down at her, wanting so much more than he could do in public. It had been a timely reminder of the promise he'd made to her, and one that could have cost them greatly. And from the look in Hope's eyes, she felt the same.

'Yes,' he said, answering her question about the

photos, and gestured with his head towards the chalet, careful to keep his hands to himself.

Luca led Hope to the greeting desk. On one side of the chalet's floor was a large canteen-style buffet where families, couples and even a ski class were busy piling plates high with delicious-smelling food, the other where tables and chairs were rapidly filling up.

Hope watched as he spoke to the waitress behind the desk, who smiled and nodded, gesturing for them to follow her up the large wooden staircase to the second floor, which opened up to a restaurant dining area. Tables covered in white cloth and silverware were half full with slightly more sedate customers than the raucous ski groups downstairs. Hope thought that they might stop there, but the waitress continued on to the balcony and, pulling back glass sliding doors, she led her and Luca out towards a private table for two. Luca thanked the waitress while Hope simply stared at the view.

Discreet outside heaters gently warmed them from above, and though only glass separated them from the dining room, there was the impression of privacy—they were alone with the view. Their chairs, covered in rich white faux fur, suited the silver, glass and green fir sprigs decorating the table. It looked like a winter wonderland but while her designer's eye appreciated the touches, it was the natural beauty of the mountains that called to her the most.

'You're spoiling me today, Luca. I'm going to have

to come up with more words than stunning, beautiful, awe-inspiring.'

She turned to find him looking at her. Really looking.

'Now you know how I feel,' he said, and her heart fluttered in her chest, replacing the earlier discomfort from the encounter with the paparazzo.

For just a moment, she'd allowed herself to forget. Forget that they couldn't be seen in public together, that the easy affection she wanted to give was not possible. Forget that this, whatever it was, had limits before it had even started.

He pulled a chair out for her and she sat, before he took the seat opposite her.

'Thank you,' she said, not knowing how much she meant it until the words left her lips. He nodded, the look in his eyes understanding, rather than dismissing what the moment meant to her. And it was novel. To be so understood.

Being a twin was a connection that was hard to explain to most people. There was a bond there that went so deep, sometimes she'd wanted to break free from it. But then Nate had collapsed and the fear she'd felt that day, the genuine, honest-to-God moment of heart-stopping, mind-blanking fear had rocked her to her core.

And though that connection blazed strong between them, she sometimes felt that Nate didn't take the time to understand her. Sending Luca after her without speaking to her, believing that she needed protection—or that she couldn't have seen to that herself, believing that she wouldn't realise that there was more to Luca than being a chauffeur, were prime examples. Perhaps even doubting that she could be CEO of Harcourts was another.

But Luca? She felt he did actually understand her. He didn't underestimate her or what she wanted or could even achieve. And it frustrated her that she didn't know the same about him. It was possible that his reticence was just with her, but Hope felt that it went deeper than that, instinctively knowing that he would be just as much of a closed book with other women.

She thought back to the other day, when they'd argued about this lifestyle.

'What kind of life is that? It's bland. It's ridiculous. You're being used for someone else's momentary fascination and you're allowing it.'

She'd never forget those words as long as she lived. And now, she realised, truly realised, he hadn't been talking about her.

Hope waited until the waitress had poured both water and wine and left before asking the question burning in her chest.

'Who is she?'

'Who?' Luca asked with a frown marring his brow.

'The person you know who lives this life.'

Her gaze took in the pulsing muscle at his jaw, the living, breathing dragon that lived behind the blank gaze he'd erected between them. His body had betrayed nothing. But the energy that pounded beneath his skin, the change in temperature between them told her so much.

He stayed silent for so long, Hope looked away. What right did she have to pry into his life? She felt foolish and embarrassed for asking, for overstepping whatever line it was—as invisible as it might be— that lay between them.

She reached for her glass and her hand nearly knocked it over when he answered.

'My mother.'

CHAPTER NINE

THE WORDS ENDED years of silence and secrecy, landing between them like an unexploded bomb. Luca's heart pounded in his chest. He'd never told anyone. Thirty-four years of keeping a secret was a hard habit to shake and even now he felt nearly sick at the thought of it.

He could see Hope trying to make a mental connection between his name and someone she knew and, when that failed, she looked at him, searching for features she might recognise. His cut glass cheekbones, the rich dark hair, the unusual silvery grey gaze.

'Oh,' she said, blinking as she put two and two together. It was his eyes. They were his mother's. Anna Bertoli, the famous Italian actress who had managed to do the unthinkable: cross from Italy to Hollywood without disdain or derision. She was a screen siren with more global recognition than Harcourts could even dream of having.

'I didn't know she had children,' Hope said, without thinking.

'She doesn't.'

Hope flinched at the cutting edge of his tone and he instantly regretted it. But the internal battle raging between wanting to protect his mother and wanting to tell her was riding him hard. Because he thought she, of all people, might understand. Hope knew the weight of the attention of the press, of the importance of reputation. And because he thought she might be able to keep his secret. Hoped that she would, because a part of him wanted someone he didn't have to lie to, someone he didn't have to keep himself separate from.

Luca's sigh was a surrender. 'There are only two other people, besides Anna and myself, that know this.' He hadn't realised it, but his palms had turned upwards, a physical manifestation of the question he didn't have to ask.

'I will never tell,' Hope promised and he—who rarely trusted anyone—believed her with absolute certainty.

'I don't see her much. I *can't*,' he said, trying to explain his very complicated feelings about the press and public life. 'Anna forged her career as an ingenue, an enigma, an alluring woman who remained dedicated only to her career and her fans. That she's not had children is part of her brand,' he said with a shrug, as if he were running down the CV of a client rather than describing his mother's achievements. In part because all of those achievements had required him to be invisible.

'She must have been incredibly young when she

had you,' Hope hedged. He knew it was a gentle probe. Something he didn't have to answer if he didn't want to.

'Sixteen.'

Hope cursed, the word almost funny in her crisp English accent. But there really was nothing funny about a pregnant single sixteen-year-old girl.

'He was a co-star, apparently.'

'Apparently?' Hope asked, her eyes getting darker and darker with an empathy that was new and unfamiliar to him.

'She never told me his name,' Luca said. Anna had, instead, told him that it had been a terrible mistake, that she wished it had never happened and that he had told her to just 'get rid of it'. If she had even realised the impact of what she was saying to her child, he'd never seen a sign of it. In Anna's world, she had simply been telling him how terrible it had been for *her*. He'd wondered once if it was a defence mechanism. If she'd *had* to see the world that way, to live with the decisions she'd made, but he didn't like to think that hard about it. Instead, what he'd clung to as a child was that she had stayed. His mother had stayed when she could so easily have not. How could a child not be thankful for that?

'At the time, her father was her agent, her mother had died a few years before. It wasn't too difficult to explain her absence by an eight-month stint on an independent film that didn't get off the ground. And after she had me, she returned to make *Il Cuore Vuole*, the film that made her an international star.

'But from that moment on, I was a threat to her,' he confessed. 'Neither Hollywood nor Italian cinema would have touched an unwed sixteen-year-old mother of one.'

Hope reached out her hand across the table and, as much as he wanted to take the comfort she offered—more than he'd ever wanted anything—he couldn't forget that they weren't in private. Just like with his mother, there were too many witnesses and something buried deep ached all over again.

She withdrew her hand, apologies in her eyes for the gesture of comfort she couldn't give.

It was strange speaking of it after all this time. For so long everything he'd thought about it, he'd felt about it, had been unspoken. Seeing the sadness for him in Hope's gaze legitimised his feelings in a way that was new for him.

He wished that didn't make him angry. He wished that he still wanted to protect his mother, the way he had been so desperate to as a child. But he wasn't a child any more. He had seen the way the world worked, and what Anna had told him then didn't make as much sense now.

'Who raised you?' she asked.

'Anna's older sister and her husband. Alma and Pietro. They'd never had children of their own and after their mother passed, they loved Anna like their own.'

But not you?

Her question might not have been spoken but he read it easily in her eyes.

He was saved from having to answer by the arrival

of the food he'd ordered before he'd lost all appetite following their conversation.

Hope seemingly felt the same way as the food went untouched long after the waitress left.

'So, you have protected her secret?' Hope asked, reaching for the water rather than the wine.

'Yes,' he said with a conviction that went deeper than any vow. No matter what their relationship was like, Anna was his mother.

'Why?' she asked tentatively, as if afraid that the question would seem rude or thoughtless, even though he knew that Hope was neither of those things.

Why? It was a question he'd been asking himself a lot in the last few years. It had made sense when he'd been a child. He'd seen himself as her knight, as Anna's protector. But was he really that same little boy, still hoping that she'd love him? That she'd finally recognise him and claim him? Something he realised in that moment, with a start, that Anna Bertoli would never do.

'But she supported you?' Hope asked in the absence of an answer, her concern that his mother had fulfilled at least some part of her maternal duties clear in her tone.

'She gave Alma and Pietro whatever they needed to raise me and, although it wasn't too much to raise suspicions, it was definitely enough. And then at eighteen there was an inheritance of sorts.'

'Of sorts?'

'Anna wanted me to have some money, but said

that her lawyers were worried about it so they tied it into a non-disclosure agreement.'

'An NDA for what?' Hope demanded, already halfway to furious on his behalf.

'That I never revealed myself as her child.'

Shock punched the breath from her lungs. Her hand flew to her mouth. 'She…' Hope couldn't find the words. In all her years at an all-girls boarding school, throughout which she genuinely thought she'd experienced some of the cruellest behaviour, and even beyond that—seeing what Simon was willing to do for power and control—none of it compared to a mother not just disowning her son, but silencing him too.

'You can do a lot with half a million,' he said, as if he felt the need to justify his choice. She realised that he was worried what she thought of him.

She desperately wanted to reach for him then. She wanted to curl up in his lap and hold him and tell him words she had no place offering him. Because he couldn't even take her hand. And she hated that she couldn't offer it to him. It made her feel unworthy of him.

'It's okay,' he assured her, as if sensing her inner battle.

'It's not,' she replied, refusing to let him excuse it, the way he clearly tried to excuse his mother's behaviour. 'And she should never have done that to you,' she whispered harshly. 'You should never have had to sign such a thing, certainly not in exchange for your silence,' she insisted, and even though it made her want to question their own agreement, this was about him and about his mother, not them. No wonder he had made a career from living in the shadows, from keeping secrets. Yes, he had become a protector, a saviour to some—she was sure. But at what cost?

'Luca you did the *right* thing by taking the money. Because you made something of your own. Something you can be proud of. And that means something. The man you have become owes nothing to that woman,' Hope said, sure of her words, but unsure whether she had the right to say such a thing.

His eyes on her were fierce. She *felt* what it meant to him to hear that. And somewhere in that molten silver unwound passion and a heat so intense she felt a flush rise to her skin. But in spite of that passion, she still needed him to know one thing.

'You shouldn't have to live in the shadows. You deserve more, Luca.'

He nodded his acceptance of her statement, not once taking his eyes from her, but she still felt that he held a part of himself back.

'Hope, no one can know,' he warned, and she knew that this wasn't a request from the wrong side of a legal agreement. It was the request of a son determined to protect his mother. And she would do anything to honour it.

They spent the rest of the afternoon chasing each other across the runs and slopes of white powdery snow. After a few forced moments of happiness to change the mood over lunch to something lighter, the lie became the truth, as if they were both determined to put the past behind them and focus only on the present. As if they were both aware that time was running out before they returned to London and would have to stop whatever this thing was between them. Because even as every part of her being wanted Luca with a ferocity that scared her almost, she knew that their relationship wouldn't, couldn't, survive the scrutiny of the press.

So after a few slopes they embraced the freedom of their movements, allowing it to lift her heart that afternoon as they sped across dramatic vistas with barely a soul to see. The sweeping sound of her skis on snow, Luca's delicious—and sometimes wicked— laughter, all standing out against the backdrop of a clear blue sky without a hint of a cloud.

She convinced Luca to let them go to one of the ski bars on the way down the mountain, promising to keep her goggles on as they shared a mulled wine and were tempted to shots of Jägermeister, the syrupy sweet alcohol with a punch. It had almost been a game, how far they could push each other without the displays of affection they both so clearly wanted.

Stomachs growling from a full day of skiing and a barely touched lunch, they sneaked into a bistro and, after securing a table in the back of the restaurant, they wolfed down *schnitzel*, and buttery greens and mashed potato for Luca and *frites* for Hope, who rarely let herself indulge in so much naughtiness in a week, let alone a day. And as the crispy, salty crunch exploded on her tongue, she began to wonder just how much she had sacrificed in becoming the face of Harcourts. As if sensing the direction of her thoughts, Luca distracted her with a forkful of garlic mushrooms that she couldn't resist.

Reluctant to make the trip back on their skis through the wooded forest in the dark, Luca arranged for a car to take them back to the chalet, from a service he trusted, and the moment they were through the front door, Luca was peeling her clothes from her body and she was frantically tugging at his. He walked them down the hall to where the spa rooms were and guided her towards the hammam.

'Shower first,' she said against his lips and he simply shook his head, pushing her onto the glass-panelled room, his urgency, his need for her pressing against her stomach, and driving her beyond rational thought.

'I've wanted to do this all day,' he growled into her ear.

He picked her up, her legs instinctively wrapping around his waist, and backed against the door so that it opened for them, pressing a button on the panel on the side that filled the room with a delicate-scented steam that brought a slick sheen to her skin in seconds. He sat with her once again on his lap, only this time he brought her leg across so that she straddled him, the thick blunt head of his penis teasing her folds.

He took her mouth in a kiss that was carnal, invasive and possessive, burning her hotter than anything the steam room was capable of. She rolled against him, her hips, her thighs, her chest, unfurling inch by inch, her entire body craving the feel of him against her.

And she was in heaven until she heard Luca curse with frustration.

'Condom,' he growled, and he pressed his forehead against hers.

For a moment Hope's mind went blank and then rushed back in a heartbeat. 'I'm on the pill. Contraception. I'm on it. And I'm clean,' she said in a rush.

He looked up at her, she could see the warring in his eyes. The desperation to be that intimate with her, but also the awareness of consequences, of mistakes. She wouldn't force this on him, it was his choice as much as it was hers. No one had the right to take that from anyone.

'I'm clean too,' he said, and she understood the incredible trust he had placed in her.

She nodded in answer to his unspoken question. She wanted this more than she wanted her next breath.

'But Hope, this is going to be hard and fast,' he warned, the wicked promise bringing a wetness to her core. In answer to his unspoken question, she rose onto her knees enough to reach between them and grip the length of his erection, hot and thick in her palm. Her thumb brushed the head of his penis, where a small bead of moisture already tipped against her finger.

'You'll be the death of me, Harcourt,' he growled against her lips, as she guided him to her entrance. His hands, one on each of her sit bones, palmed the backs of her thighs, spreading her for him, his fingers dipping into her folds.

'You're so wet, *cara*,' he said.

'That's what you do to me,' she whispered into his ear, before sinking down onto the steel of him as he rose up to meet her with a powerful thrust that drew a cry from her lips.

She spread her knees wider, sinking just that bit more onto him, and felt him pulse deep against her core. Her head fell against his shoulder, a sob exploding from her chest. With one arm around her waist and the other pinning her chest to his, he withdrew slowly, a delicious torture, before slamming back into her with a guttural cry. Bracing herself against his shoulders as he held her just slightly above him, again and again he pounded into her, forcing her towards an orgasm she wasn't sure she'd survive. Luca filled her so completely, she felt all of him as he moved within her, but when he found that little rough patch of nerves hidden deep within her, Luca hitting it again and again until he became so hard, so steely within her, it felt alchemical.

'I've got you,' he whispered as he thrust into her again. 'I've got you. You can let go,' he said.

As if that was what she'd been waiting to hear her entire life, she gave in, standing in the path of the orgasm building between them as it crashed down on them like a tidal wave and all she could do was surrender.

Luca had never come so hard in his entire life. Aftershocks still burst through his body, even as he picked up a thoroughly ravished Hope and walked them into the shower stall. Turning on the spray of warm water, he lathered his hands in the shower gel and gently began to wash her body. She felt delicate under his touch, but he knew the strength of this woman—even if perhaps she wasn't always sure of it herself. Lust-drunk dark eyes watched him as he ran soapy hands gently between her legs, caressing and cleansing as he went.

After seeing to himself, and before he could become even more of a neanderthal and take her again in the shower, he turned off the water, dried them off and wrapped her in a large fluffy white robe.

'Where are we going?' she asked as he led her out of the ground floor and towards the fourth.

It was a good question, and even though he replied, 'Upstairs,' his mind threw up many different answers to the same question. But what he wanted and what he could have were two different things. They always had been. Hope's life—so prominently in the public eye—was impossible for him. Within an hour of being seen together there would be deep dives into his background, his family. There would be photos and research, and while Anna Bertoli on paper had no connection to Luca Calvino, he knew it wouldn't take too much digging, too much work to uncover the truth. The only reason it hadn't been done before now was because of his anonymity. So the only answer his mind offered to her question was *Nowhere*, even as everything in him roared in denial. This, whatever it was, had an expiration date. But until then he would satiate every single craving or desire Hope Harcourt could conceive of.

He went to a cupboard and produced a very nice bottle of red while Hope retrieved the glasses. Hitting the buttons on the solar-powered heaters, having stored their energy through the day, he flooded the balcony with gentle warmth and a subtle glow. He flicked a button on the hot tub and Hope started to laugh.

'You're trying to turn me into a prune, Calvino,' she said, the lightness of her tone soothing his concern that he'd been too rough with her.

He turned, apparently, the question clear in his gaze.

She put down the glasses on the small table beside the bubbling tub. 'That was incredible,' she said, walking into his space, slipping her hands between the robe he wore and pressing herself against him like a cat. She reached up to cup his jaw. 'You gave me what I wanted before I knew to ask for it,' she said, easing any concern he'd had about what they had just shared. He kissed her, letting his relief, his thanks and his promises for more to come, bleed into the kiss.

'A prune, Calvino,' she teased, pulling back from the kiss, giving them both the chance to breathe.

She shrugged out of her robe, gloriously and utterly unselfconsciously naked as she stepped into the frothing bubbles of the hot tub. Lithe and graceful, and he'd have known that even if he hadn't spent the entire day watching her traversing the slopes and runs as if she'd been born to them.

Shucking his own robe, he joined her in the bubbling heat, steam rising around them and disappearing into the night sky.

Although the kiss had rekindled the arousal between them, the burning desire that had driven him almost the entire day had been sated enough for him to simply enjoy the feel of her next to him, to luxuriate in the easy touches that passed between them as they settled into their wine, talking of particular slopes or moments of the day they'd enjoyed. And although the conversation was easy, he knew that the revelation about his mother had left an imprint. It made him think of the anniversary of her parents' death. Of how she'd spent that night alone and he wished he'd had enough sense to fight her harder on that.

'What were your parents like?' he asked, wondering if she'd shut him down, hoping that she wouldn't.

She looked out at the view of the mountains and was quiet for so long he thought she wouldn't answer.

'Busy,' she said, surprising him with the choice of word. 'Harcourts is from Dad's side of the family, and he was groomed to take over from grandfather. Not something I think my uncle enjoyed very much. Perhaps that's why Simon is so determined to become CEO.' She smiled pensively. 'But they were busy. Mum was an interior designer.'

'Where you get your eye from?' Luca enquired.

She smiled up at him, as if thrilled he'd noticed.

'I'd like to think so. She filled the house with colour, prints and paintings, everything that was bright and cool. She would take kitsch and make it classy, and would get lost in a fabric shop the same way others might get lost in a museum,' Hope said, smiling. 'We actually did that once. Got lost in a fabric shop. I would swear, even now, it took us nearly the entire day to find our way out.'

She grinned up at Luca, the memory pulled to the surface by his question, of that special, magical moment in time when it had just been the two of them. 'Nate was off with Dad, probably at Harcourts, but Mum and I spent the day pulling out reams of bright fabric and soft textures, sequins and silks.'

Her mother had promised to make her a dress for her twelfth birthday from the material they bought that day, but…then the accident had happened. Hope didn't remember seeing the material again. After the funeral their grandfather had closed down the house, put most of their parents' things in storage, sold the family townhouse in London and put the money into the trust fund that both Hope and Nate had access to when they turned twenty-one.

'And your father?'

The question pulled Hope to another memory. 'Tall,' she said instantly, remembering clinging to his leg and looking up at him as he reached down to pick her up. 'He had a bit of a temper, would shout, and of the two, we were definitely more scared of him than our mother. But she would soften him, soothe him. Coffee makes me think of him,' she said softly. 'And caramel makes me think of her.'

'How did they meet?' Luca asked, pulling her closer to him to rub soothing circles at her neck.

'She had been working as an assistant to a window dresser, but he was temperamental and had an artistic disagreement with Grandfather, who promptly ordered Mum to 'fix it'. That's the story they always told, anyway.'

'So Harcourts was the centre of everything?'

It was the heart.

'Mum worked there before having us and then, after we were old enough, took on some private interior design clients. But Nate and I grew up in the halls of Harcourts. Playing hide and seek before it opened and after it closed, waiting for Mum and Dad to finish up work. All the staff knew us. It used to be a family joke that the store was the biggest nursery in the world.

'Dad would sneak Nate into the board meetings sometimes,' she remembered.

'And you?'

'I would be outside with the secretaries,' Hope replied, losing a little of that smile. 'They were lovely, but busy. I sometimes wondered if less work was done in the meetings than outside of it.'

Luca nodded. 'Probably quite true.'

She turned to him to prise a kiss from his lips, trying to remove that anxious, uncomfortable feeling when she remembered things like that. Luca indulged her, but she realised it was precisely that. An indulgence that lacked the punch of heat she felt when he wanted her.

'He was grooming Nate even then?' Luca asked eventually when she came up for air.

Hope shrugged, not enjoying the questions now.

'I don't know,' she replied.

'Yes, you do,' Luca pushed, not unkindly. 'But he was a man with values imparted from an older man. And you were children with fully formed personalities and half-formed dreams.'

She wanted to push back at him, at his perceptiveness.

'You should forgive him,' he urged gently.

'For what?' she replied, despite knowing full well where Luca was leading her.

'He couldn't have known.'

'Known what?'

'How much you would love Harcourts. How much it's in your blood,' he said, taking her hand and pressing a kiss to the pulse at her wrist.

'Of course I do. It's—'

'Nate has three other companies,' Luca observed. 'And?'

'You don't,' he stated. 'Your brother loves *business*. You love Harcourts. And you have every right, if not more, to that CEO position. Even if you don't believe it yet.'

The unearthing of her vulnerability was painful and raw. She hated that she was jealous of her twin, hated that she had been angry with her father as a child, angry before she'd even really been able to put a word to the swirling emotion that had heated her cheeks and made her heart ache. And she hated that she wanted Harcourts so much that she'd do almost anything to get it.

Luca was right. She loved it with every ounce of her being.

He reached for her and Hope went to him willingly, to kneel in the space he made for her between his legs. Yes, there was arousal there, attraction that seemed almost constantly to simmer beneath the surface, but comfort was what she sought, and what Luca gave her when she most needed it.

CHAPTER TEN

THE CALL FROM Sofia Obeid had come in early the next morning and the air around Hope had been electrified ever since. Luca drove them to where Hope had arranged to meet Sofia, unnervingly happy that it wasn't another club and didn't involve another man to disguise the meeting. He peered through the wide window of the restaurant that was nearly half full of diners. This far from the slopes in Hallstatt, it was a classy establishment for those who wanted something away from the crowds of tourists.

The winding drive into the picturesque valley, down to the lake nestled in the basin of mountains, had failed to distract Hope from typing notes furiously into her phone. He'd asked her if she knew what she was going to say. She'd nodded, her fingers halting on the screen for just a moment, and then she'd nodded again and gone back to typing.

'Are you sure about meeting here? It's very public. I can't control photographers here,' he warned.

'I'm done with hiding, Luca. I'm done with pretending to be less than I am,' she said, her tone determined in a way that made him proud and pleased at the same time.

'Do you want me to come in with you?' he asked.

'No,' she said with a smile as she opened the door before he could even think of doing it for her.

He watched her cross the road and, even though he was parked in a no parking zone, he refused to move the car away from where he could see her. She entered the restaurant and a waiter took her to a table that was thankfully still in the view of the window.

He recognised the woman who stood up from the table, greeting Hope warmly, as the same woman who had left the club the night before last, tall, striking and slightly older than Hope. He wondered if the people in the restaurant had any idea of the power that these two women had at their fingertips.

He'd cast an eye over Hope's plan while she'd been preparing and while he didn't understand the specifics, he knew enough about numbers to know that the board and the shareholders would be absolutely out of their minds to ignore a deal that could net them nearly half a billion pounds in profit by the second year of the branded hotels' opening. It was clever. It was daring. It was global, and Luca had absolutely no doubt in his mind that it would work.

He just couldn't work out how she didn't know it. How she didn't know how brilliant she was. He wanted to throttle her brother and shake her grandfather. These were the people who were supposed to protect her and raise her with a confidence and self-assurance that she deserved.

Watching her sit down opposite Sofia Obeid, Luca realised that he didn't want this to end here, in Austria. Yes, there was a huge amount on the line if they even tried to continue a relationship moving forward—his business deal, avoiding the press, Anna…

These weren't inconsiderable things to him. He'd spent his entire life protecting his mother's reputation and he'd spent his entire adult life protecting and developing his own business. It was the one thing, the *one* thing, that grounded him in this world. The one thing that would prove he'd ever been here.

But a reckless, demanding part of him didn't want to give Hope up. He—who trusted almost no one—had trusted her with more of himself than he'd ever shown anyone. And he knew that he'd seen a side of Hope that no one else had ever seen, not even that bastard of an ex-fiancé.

His mind scrabbled to make the scenario work. Clandestine meetings, illicit encounters, ways around attracting the attention of the press… He'd do it, he realised. He'd do that for her. He could even see himself giving up the contract that Nate Harcourt had dangled in front of him like a carrot to protect Hope in the first place. He would stay in the shadows for her, like he had done for his mother.

And he didn't know whether that terrified him because it was a good thing, or because it was the worst thing.

'Thank you so much for making the time,' Hope said, surprised that she wasn't feeling nervous. The urgency and desperation that had driven her in their last meeting was strangely absent.

'I'm glad I was able to,' Sofia replied sincerely, her gaze assessing, as if noting the change in Hope too.

'I don't have any changes to the offer. I can't and, to be honest, even if I could, I *wouldn't* make any changes to what is already both a good idea and a good deal for us both.'

Sofia frowned slightly, her only outward sign of confusion about where this conversation might be going then. Hope didn't want to waste either of their time with unnecessary platitudes.

'But I did want to give you another answer to the question you asked before, about why I wanted this. If I'm honest,' Hope admitted, 'I wasn't aware of what was driving me then. And in some ways, if you hadn't forced me to question it, I might never have realised it, so I'd like to thank you.'

Sofia's eyes were impassive, but Hope didn't care. If the amazing businesswoman sitting opposite her didn't get it or understand—even as she prayed that wasn't the case—Hope realised that she'd find another way. Because she loved Harcourts and because she loved what she did. And she *would* find a way of making it hers.

'At the beginning I thought that I was trying to make this deal because it would wrestle the CEO position away from my cousin. I thought I was doing it for my brother, who had been groomed from childhood to become the CEO, first by my father and then my grandfather. I thought that I could maybe caretake it for him, until he returns, paying him back for all the times that he protected me after my parents died.'

Sympathy and a hint of understanding flared in Sofia's gaze.

'But... I don't want to give it away,' she said, finally admitting the truth out loud. 'I want the CEO position for myself. And I want this deal because it's an *excellent* idea, it's an *exciting* idea, and because it's *my* idea. I can see it so clearly in my mind, I can almost feel the gold handle of the hotel door, with our names across the top of it,' she said, conjuring the images in her mind as she said them. 'I want this because Harcourts is my legacy and my future. Because I want to thrust it into the twenty-first century, with new designers and a socially conscious ethos. I want Harcourts to speak to, not *down* to, the communities that it supplies,' she said, nearly out of breath with the passion pulsing through her body with every beat of her heart.

There was so much more she could have said, but Hope realised she didn't need to as she looked at Sofia smiling back at her with satisfaction and an excitement of her own.

'*Now* you are someone I would like to do business with,' Sofia stated confidently.

'I can't lie, I'm not the CEO yet.'

Sofia nodded, clearly debating what she was about to say. 'Hope, if they choose Simon over you, then you might have to think about leaving. Because as much as you love that business, it will never love you back.'

'But you're agreeing to the deal,' Hope said, re-

fusing to let Sofia's warning dim the bright shining
light building in her chest.

Sofia smiled. 'Did you bring the paperwork?'

Hope managed to contain her excitement until she
got back into the SUV and turned to Luca.

'You did it,' he said, a smile splitting his handsome features, his steely grey eyes bright with silvery sparks.

She didn't answer. Instead, she grabbed him and
kissed him hard and hot and deep, her hands pulling
him to her meeting no resistance. She clung to the
kiss, desperately almost, praying that Luca wouldn't
notice—that she couldn't speak, couldn't think past
the fear of how much him being there had meant to
her. How much she'd wanted *him* to know that she'd
got the deal. Not her brother, not her grandfather—
the people she had spent her life wanting to impress,
but Luca—who had come to mean so much to her in
such a short space of time. Too much, she realised, as
she responded to the pounding of his heart beneath
the palm of her hand, where it rested on his chest.

He pulled back from the kiss, breath punching in
and out of his chest. 'I'm taking you home,' he said,
and she knew she should correct him, that the chalet
wasn't their home, but the words stuck in her throat,
the fiery passion blazing in his gaze setting her body
alight with that very same need.

Luca didn't know how many speed limits he broke on
the way home, and Hope hardly helped matters. She

couldn't keep her hands off him, her palm smoothing over his thigh muscle, dangerously close to where he really wanted her.

She looked at him, and where he'd once seen disinterest and aloofness, he now saw so much more. He saw need, raw and unvarnished, in the swirls of espresso and heated caramel, making his whole body pulse with a thick arousal he feared he might never satiate.

All he knew was that by the time they pulled into the driveway to the chalet he was ready to claim her in a way that was primal and powerful, in a way he'd never experienced before. Which was why he kept his hands on the steering wheel, trying to claw back some sense of control.

He felt her gaze on him. 'Luca—'

'I need a minute,' he said, concerned by the intensity of his need for her, concerned about what that could lead to.

'I don't,' she replied.

'Hope…' Her name was a plea and a warning at the same time.

'I can see it,' she said. 'How much you want me.'

Clenching his jaw, he forced himself to meet her gaze.

'Don't you see that same want in me? That same ferocity? I want you like *this*,' she said, her words a silvery seduction enticing him to his deepest needs, as she leaned towards him, her lips already partway open when she pressed against his mouth, inviting his tongue, his hands, his heart…

This was Hope emboldened and she was magnificent. She shifted across the console, too impatient to wait, his hands reaching for the lever to pull the seat back in time for her to straddle his thighs, and too fast for him to explain that the chalet was just there.

Her kisses drugged him. Her hands reached between them, found his painfully hard erection and her palms teased more than soothed the heat between his legs. Unable to fight it any more, he reached for her, his hands wrapping around her, holding her in place above him, her blonde hair hanging around them like a halo.

He teased her breasts with his thumbs, the arch of her back pressing them closer to where he wanted, and he pressed open-mouthed kisses over the thin merino knit top she was wearing, the stiff peaks of her nipples punched against wool damp from his attention. He let her go, knowing she'd support herself, and reached between her legs, the same damp heat there just from her pleasure.

'Please,' Hope whimpered, rocking herself back and forth across his lap, his erection and his sanity. The wrap-over cashmere skirt she wore had slipped either side of his lap, showing slivers of perfectly smooth trembling thighs. Gasps shuddering through her, her hand reached between her thighs to ease her own need, but he pulled it away, pressing kisses into her palm, and growled the words, 'Not yet.' Her eyes flared, the pulsing in them matching the throbbing in his groin.

'Luca,' she cried from need and want.

Biting back a curse, he freed himself from his trousers, reached between the heaven of her legs, pulled aside the damp silk, sweat already beading at the base of his spine and the last coherent thought he had before he thrust into the hot, wet heat of her was that if this was madness, he never wanted to be sane again.

Hope's gasp of raw pleasure filled the car as she braced her palm against the roof, to push herself back down onto each thrust. He could feel the twitch of her muscles as they encased him, gripping him. She was already as close as he was.

Breath punched in and out of his chest as he fought to hold off the impending orgasm building deep within him. His hands palmed the underside of her trembling thighs, holding her in place as he pounded into her from beneath, his hips thrusting and pulse racing.

Instinct took over, and any concern that it was too fast, too hard, fled as Hope's desperate cries urged him on. He reached for the hand she had on his shoulder and moved it between them, his finger guiding hers against her clitoris.

Her eyes sought his, filled with so much dark desire and a desperate want.

'Now, *cara*,' he said, and watched with his heart in his mouth as she began to touch herself. Her head fell back as she gave herself over to the pleasure they were making together. She coated him as he withdrew from her agonisingly, only to thrust back into her with a dizzying force. She took everything but gave him more.

Luca raced against their impending orgasm, desperate to wring as much pleasure from this moment as possible, determined to hear one more pleasure-filled cry fall from her lips, to feel her grip him once more as he pulsed deep within her. To take one more breath through an arousal that made the air thick and fogged the windows. His thighs slapped against hers again and again as he pounded deep into her, as he felt her fingertips from where she brought herself closer and closer until they lost the fight and she came apart around him, drawing his own orgasm from deeper than he'd ever felt before.

It was the most intense orgasm Hope had ever had. She had let Luca carry her from the car and into the shower on the ground floor, and somehow he'd then taken her to their bed, where she'd fallen into a bliss-filled unconsciousness.

So when she heard the buzz from her mobile phone it took her a moment to try and orientate herself. She wasn't even sure what the time was. The room was dark and her screen so bright she squinted to see the name.

She blinked awake in an instant. Unplugging it from where it was charging, she slipped from the bed, hoping not to wake Luca. She tiptoed out of the room and upstairs to the fourth floor.

'What do you want?' she demanded when she finally hit the accept button on the call.

'Can't I just give my little cousin a call, now? Have we become such adversaries?'

'Simon, drop the crap. I don't have time for this.'

'No, I'm sure you don't,' he said insidiously.

Everything in her went still. He wouldn't call unless he had something. He wouldn't call unless he thought he'd already won. Her stomach turned in on itself.

'What do you want?' she repeated, not quite trusting herself to say anything else.

'Nothing. In fact, it's entirely the opposite. I have something for you,' he said, his tone overly civil. 'I managed to obtain something I thought you might be interested in. Check your inbox. I'll wait.'

She put the call on hold while she pulled up her inbox on her phone. His email was waiting for her, but when she clicked on the attachment she nearly dropped her phone.

There were several pictures of her and Luca, taken when they had been in the hot tub only the day before. One of her in his lap, another of them kissing, and one of him looking at her as if he wanted to devour her. Her pulse rocketed and her skin stung, the violation of their privacy absolutely horrifying.

The photographer Luca had warned off, she guessed. If he'd been freelancing for the press, she wouldn't have seen these pictures until they were beneath a headline. The fact that Simon had them could only mean that he'd been the one to hire the photographer.

She bit back the wave of nausea turning her stomach, her mind racing, Although the pictures bordered on explicit, she didn't doubt there were worse ones she hadn't been sent. In an instant she saw it—realised what these photographs meant and her heart jerked in her chest. The press might be interested in who Luca was, but Simon would be a bloodhound. He wouldn't stop until he knew everything, in the hope that it would give him leverage to get what he wanted.

She closed down the email app and opened another on her phone and, after arranging what she wanted, she took the call off hold.

'What do you want, Simon?' she bit out, not even bothering to suppress the rage she felt in that moment. She was almost certain she knew, but she needed him to say it.

'Let's not be coy about this,' he snarled into the phone. 'I know you have some kind of deal on the table in an attempt to woo the shareholders into voting for you in two days' time. But I doubt any deal would trump another sex scandal from you.'

'There hasn't even been one sex scandal,' she growled into the phone.

'Oh, I'm sure your ex-fiancé has something up his sleeve, if this doesn't do the trick. I want you to back out of the CEO vote, or I'll start digging. Because though you may be egalitarian, you wouldn't be sleeping with the help, Hope. So, while I don't yet know who he is, it's only a matter of time.'

Luca paused at the top of the stairs. He'd woken just as Hope slipped from the room and he'd worried when she hadn't come back. He watched her pace the living room floor, whispering harshly into the phone.

He couldn't quite hear her, but it was clear something was wrong. He frowned, and debated whether to go to her, but he could tell from her body language that it might not be a good idea. The call wrapped up and she turned to stare at the darkness through the window.

Quietly, he returned to the room and the bed and waited.

When Hope tiptoed in about half an hour later, he lifted the cover for her.

'Everything okay?' he asked.

'Absolutely,' she said, smiling back at him, not re-alising that her one word had eviscerated him. And neither of them slept again that night.

The next morning Hope packed her things while Luca was in the shower, stomach churning and heart ach-ing.

She knew what she had to do, and that it hurt so much to do it only served to make Hope even more convinced that it was the right thing. Time and time again she'd seen that she could only trust herself; look what had happened with Martin, and wasn't she just making the same mistake in trying to rely on Luca? It wasn't as if they had a future beyond Austria anyway.

Just until we return.

Had she said that? Or had it been Luca? She threw a jumper into the suitcase angrily. That she didn't even remember, didn't know, just went to prove how much being with Luca confused things for her. And she couldn't afford to be confused right now. Her focus *had* to be on Harcourts, on beating Simon.

Yes, Simon had sent a photographer after her, but *she* was the one who had drawn Luca into the mess of her family struggles. The least she could do was ensure that Luca and his mother didn't get caught in the crossfire.

But if Luca knew what Simon had sent to her personal email, Hope knew that he'd try to find a way to protect her. He'd not stop until he'd protected her— whatever the cost to himself. And she *couldn't* allow that to happen. It was time that someone finally protected him for a change. Even if it broke both of them to do it.

She stopped pacing back and forth across the floor when she heard his footsteps on the staircase. She'd made them coffee and when he emerged she gestured to where it was on the counter. Luca closed the distance between them and reached for the coffee, his eyes flicking between her and her suitcase, his expression inscrutable.

'I've been thinking about when I get back to London. The vote is in two days' time and things will be crazy after that, if—*when*—I get the CEO position,' she said, the words ash on her tongue. 'It's going to be a while until I might be able to see you again.'

That unfathomable gaze was locked on her, as if he knew she was lying. But she wasn't, was she? That was the thing. She would be busy when she got back, no matter what happened with the vote. And nothing changed the fact that even if she could have a relationship with him, the press would still be there. They would still want to know about Luca, who he was, what he did, where he came from. Every single inch of his personal life would be scrutinised, and nothing could protect him and his mother from that.

'I'll wait.'

'You can't,' she said, retreating into herself, pulling the layers of polite civility over her once again. It had been a mask that Luca had stripped from her, but to protect him—to protect herself—she needed to put it on once again.

'Don't do this,' he commanded, and she struggled against the order, hating the anger in his eyes, barely masking the hurt that lay beneath it. 'Don't shut me out like she did.' His words eviscerated her. Knowing how much that had not only cost him to say, but also to feel. She was rejecting him, just like his mother, and that cut something deep in her. A wound in her conscience and her soul that wouldn't heal.

'Hope,' he said, her name on his lips so different to the way he'd said it last night. The night before that. No, this time it was pain. 'You don't have to do this,' he said.

'You're right. I don't have to. But it's what I'm choosing to do, Luca. This stays here in Austria. Just like we agreed. And when I'm made CEO, I'll honour the agreement my brother made with you too. But this,' she said, gesturing between them, 'this was never going to be anything more than a pleasant distraction.'

She saw it then, her words hit their target, striking dead centre, and it did something to her. No, they'd not shared words of love, and yes, she was pushing him away as hard as she could. But it was so desperately painful that he was able to believe her so easily.

Fury coursed through his veins, blotting out rational thought and reason. Blotting out the memory of her pacing back and forth on the phone the night before.

Fury, the lash end of the whip of pain that was racking his body in a way he'd not even begun to feel just yet. He was so angry he wanted to shake her. He knew that there was something wrong with her words, with the way she said them, but he could barely see past the fact that she was walking away from him, cutting the ties that had bound them so deeply he thought he'd lost his heart.

Fool. Bloody fool.

It was happening again. Another woman turning away from him. His mother couldn't be seen with him, Hope didn't want to. The walls came slamming down, cutting off everything but the ice that was forming around his heart.

'You didn't even give it a chance, did you?' he bit out, shaking his head. Hurt and self-recrimination descended in a red haze. 'Because that's too scary for you, isn't it, Hope?' He tutted and turned away, bracing his hands on his hips. 'Fine,' he said to himself, nodding once before looking back to her. 'This? It's done. As you wish.' His hand was a slash through the air, drawing an immovable line. 'But Hope? Know that you will never be loved the way you need and want, until you're ready to open yourself up to the possibility of being hurt.'

She flinched at his words and he couldn't even bring himself to feel like the bastard he knew he was.

'I'll take you to the airport and my team will pick you up in London.'

'I've called a car. It's better if we—'

'I'm taking you to the airport,' he growled, nothing but ice in his tone. 'My team will continue in my absence until the vote, and until you can arrange for your own security.' He went to the top of the stairs where her bags were. 'I'll be in the car,' he said, picking them up on his way out of the chalet.

They drove in complete silence, Hope returning to the back seat, which he was thankful for. He wanted to shake her, he wanted to push her, he wanted her with him and he wanted her as far away from him as possible. He couldn't trust himself to speak, anger and hurt were riding him so hard.

They arrived at the airport and he opened the car door for her, Hope hiding behind her large sunglasses once again. Each step she took felt like a punch to the gut. Each second she refused to look at him, acknowledge him, another cut of the knife. And he welcomed them, reminding himself that this was why he should have kept his distance. This was how he made sure he learned his lesson this time.

He stayed by the car as the steps were pulled up, refusing to move from his post as the small jet taxied to the runway. He thought he could see Hope in one of the round windows, but told himself it was probably just his imagination. He stayed by the car as the jet powered across the tarmac, lifting delicately into the air, and he stayed by the car long after the plane became less than a dot on a denim blue sky that he hated more than he'd hated anything in his life before.

Afterwards, Hope didn't remember the flight back to London. She knew that she'd stared blindly through the cabin window with one thing on her mind.

Don't cry. Don't cry. Don't cry.

When she climbed down the stairs from the jet, a uniformed driver had the car door open for her and Hope slid into the back seat.

She absolutely refused to break in front of one of Luca's employees, even though her mind played her a collage of all the moments she'd shared with him. The way he'd looked at her in the rear-view mirror as he drove, the way he'd stopped the lift and given her his shirt. The way he'd kissed her that first time in Meister, and the way that he'd held her in the hot tub when she'd needed it.

It was all and none of those things at the same time. Her heart felt bruised and raw and hurt in a way she had never experienced before. Not even when she'd discovered the truth about Martin. Because she'd never loved her ex-fiancé the way he'd expected her to. And at first he'd wanted her for that almost as much as he'd wanted her for her money. But the fact she gave him neither of those things had enraged him.

The only thing that had angered Luca was when she was in danger, from the press or from not being true to herself. He had seen beyond every mask she'd

worn, every distraction she'd used, every wall she'd
erected, and found her. The real her. The one who was
still scared that she'd not live up to what her daddy
had wanted. Until that very last moment, when he'd
seen what she'd wanted him to see. And perhaps what
he'd expected to see all along.

She shook her head, physically trying to break
away from the direction of her thoughts, because if
she looked too closely she'd hear it. The refrain in her
soul, telling her that she loved Luca, that she adored
him, and that only made it harder to push him away.

Tears pressed at the corners of her eyes and she
willed them back. Just a little bit longer. She could
hold on just a little bit longer. Her heart was ach-
ing and she felt more alone than she'd ever felt before. Through the car window, the streets of London
looked grey and dirty. All she saw were the piles of
rubbish waiting to be collected, and the drunks and
the homeless who slept in doorways. It was the seedy
underbelly of the glitz and glamour that Harcourts'
customers paid exorbitant amounts to erase. And she
felt it—the slick grime over her skin, choking her with
the agreement she'd made with Simon.

*'You will never be loved the way you need and
want, until you're ready to open yourself up to the
possibility of being hurt.'*

Hope shook her head at Luca's parting words to
her, believing that she didn't need the love he taunted
her with. She didn't need anyone. She never had. She

could do this on her own, she thought, sweeping away the tear that had escaped.

'Ma'am, the press are at the entrance to your building.'

Hope nodded her understanding.

The driver's wary gaze looked back at her in the rear-view mirror.

'Would you like to use the garage?'

'No, thank you.'

I'm done hiding.

CHAPTER ELEVEN

LUCA TURNED THE glass in his hands, the ice sliding around the curve, lubricated by the last mouthful of whisky. He'd nursed one drink for half an hour and was considering ordering another and getting a cab back from the airport. Or maybe he could call one of his staff.

He found a bitter irony in the fact that, of all places, the meet had to happen here in Switzerland, where it had all started. He glared out at the passengers waiting for flights from behind dark glasses. The waiter had been casting nervous glances his way from the moment he'd sat down. His female colleague, however, looked like she wanted to devour him.

He rolled his shoulders and cracked his neck. The solid fist gripping his stomach since Hope had left Austria yesterday hadn't let up. He rubbed his hand across the beginnings of a beard that he might or might not keep.

He caught the commotion from the corner of his eye, the flash of bulbs and the raised voices, and for the first time in his life he didn't connect it with his mother—but Hope. He shoved back at the kneejerk jolt of concern. He clenched his jaw and ordered another whisky. He was receiving updates from his staff in London and that was all that he had now.

The glass door to the private lounge opened and in glided Anna Bertoli, her entourage staying behind to block the frenzy. Luca knew the drill by now, they had it down to an art form—almost like two dancers performing practised moves. He got up from the bar and chose an empty table with several others, equally bare, around it.

Without a glance in his direction, Anna went to the bar, ordered her drink and took a seat at a nearby table with her back practically to him.

She was a beautiful woman, his mother. Her hair was a waterfall of ebony silk falling down her back in perfect waves. Her skin was perfect, as smooth as it had always been, and he nearly laughed at the bitter irony that it was probably the most natural thing about her.

'You look well,' he said, facing away from her.

That was how they did this. Two strangers talking out at the world, rather than to each other. In a paparazzo's photograph he would just be a hazy background figure; in a fan's memory he wouldn't even appear.

'So do you,' his mother observed, even though she had yet to actually look his way. 'Is everything okay? I was surprised to get your request to meet,' she said, and he wondered whether she was really worried about him or herself.

'Do you regret it?' It wasn't what he'd planned to ask, but the words came unbidden to his lips.

Anna froze, the moment so quick it was almost imperceptible, but he'd been watching, waiting to see it and, now that he had, he wasn't sure how it made him feel. She exhaled slowly, as if through pain, and he hated that he couldn't trust that she was being truthful.

'Every day,' she replied.

'Would you have made a different choice?'

'No.' The word was a bullet that hit its mark. 'We are who we are because of our choices, Luca.' That he believed. 'And you were a child. I was trying to protect you.' The words were right, but Luca honestly thought in that moment that his mother was talking about herself.

He bit down on a chunk of ice, watering down the whisky in his empty stomach.

'The press intensity would have been truly awful for you.'

'Then.'

'Pardon?'

'Then. As a child, it would have been awful then. I'm a man now and I can take whatever you think they might throw at me.'

'Even your agreement to sign an NDA?'

Bile twisted his stomach.

'They'd eat us alive. The mother who hid her son and the son who sold his silence?'

Rage tore through him at the thought that his mother would even try to use that against him. He'd agonised over that decision—between money he desperately needed, and what…? Because there hadn't been an alternative offer that was anything other than what he already had. There hadn't been promises to recognise him in her life. There had been no exchange. It had been a payment, pure and simple. Any last hope of a familial bond frayed beneath the weight of that recognition and a line appeared in the sand, between him and her. Anna shifted in her chair as if sensing it.

'Is this because of the girl?'

This time, *he* froze.

'Hope Harcourt?'

'How do you—?'

'I saw you in the background on the front page. Even when you try not to, you stand out, you know,' his mother said with an edge to her tone that sounded a little too much like jealousy. 'Even in the shadows.'

Luca shook his head at her choice of words as they struck a chord with similar ones Hope had said over lunch in Austria. Hope had lashed out, had been angry that his mother had wanted him to stay in the shadows. She'd said as much. And Hope would also have known that being with her would do exactly the same—force him to remain there, in the darkness, to keep his promise to his mother.

Like a fist to the gut, Luca realised that Hope had been lying to him that last day in Austria. That there had been something else instigating their separation. Something that must have been tied to the phone call she'd taken that last night.

And he'd allowed himself to believe her lies because he was scared. Scared by the power of his feelings for her, by his need—yes—but by the all-consuming love he felt for her too. Scared because he feared, even now, that Hope might not think him worth the risk.

I'm done with hiding.

He could have laughed at himself right then, and not with humour. Hope Harcourt had more strength and determination than anyone he knew. Now it was time for him to prove that he was worthy of such an incredible woman.

'Luca?'

'I didn't mind it, you know,' he said, even as his mind raced towards what he needed to do next. 'Being in the shadows for you. It was safe, for us both really. You got to keep your greatest acting role, that of the eternal ingenue, and I never had to ask you to prove your love.'

Anna Bertoli might have paled, or it could have been a trick of the airport lounge lighting.

'But Hope deserves more than that. She deserves someone who will stand by her side, and I deserve that too,' he said, standing up from the table. 'Get your staff ready, Anna. It won't take long for people to put two and two together.'

'I'm sorry,' she attempted.

'I'm sorry too. But I'm sure you'll find a way to spin it to your advantage. After all, you're about to begin promoting your new film.'

Luca left the airport and hailed a car. After giving the driver instructions, he contacted the analyst on Hope's case and asked them to look into the call that Hope had received that night. He had a suspicion he already knew, but he wanted confirmation before he did anything that might jeopardise the vote being held tomorrow in London.

His heart pounded so hard in his chest, powered by a forceful combination of self-recrimination and fear. Fear that it was too late. He never should have believed what she was saying. And the words he'd said to her that last time in the chalet had been terrible. He punched a fist against his thigh. *Bastardo*.

How could he have been so stupid? Hope had spent almost her entire life going it alone—unable to trust people, unable to count on people. And he'd gone and proved her right. He, who had fallen so hard and so fast in love with her he'd not even realised it.

Well, he wasn't going to make the same mistake again. If Hope thought she could shake him off that easily, she had another think coming. And this time he was going to bring reinforcements. Hope was about to face the biggest challenge of her life, and Luca was going to make damn sure she wasn't going to do it alone.

Hope had skipped her early morning workout for this. And as much as she disliked being off her routine, she also knew that she needed it. Her driver had dropped her off in the garage, and the cleaning crew had watched her as she'd stepped out onto the floor.

There was a smell to a department store. Clean,

fresh—all carefully manufactured, but this was unique to Harcourts. Her heels clicked against the floor, echoing in the silence. The subdued pre-opening lighting made the shadows deeper and the sense of expectation greater. As if the store was holding its breath before opening time, when doors would be sprung open and streams of people would fill the aisles. Hope couldn't help but wonder if there was a sense that it was waiting for more today. Waiting to see who would stand at its helm and guide it forward into the future.

Was she doing the right thing? she asked herself.

She could only hope so.

She was putting all of her dreams and wants in one basket. Well, all but one, at least. She passed the perfume counters, the make-up stations, the cosmetics shelves and the skincare stalls. She reached out to adjust an expensive handmade Italian leather handbag on a tower of luxury purses and bags. She caught sight of the tie displays near the shirts—just a taster of what the men's section would offer on the third floor, and wondered what people would think of her plans for a non-gendered clothing section.

As she came towards the centre of the ground floor, in her mind she heard her eight-year-old self laughing as Nate chased her around the empty store. In the famous arch that had been used in at least three romantic comedy films, she saw her father kiss her mother under the mistletoe. She felt her grandfather's watchful gaze from the top floor, as he would stand there surveying his kingdom. A kingdom she wanted to inherit so badly it hurt.

But not enough to override the hurt caused by Luca's absence. One day she might be able to go to him. To explain. One day when she wasn't a threat to him and what he guarded. But not today. No, today would decide her future. And it was one she would meet head-on.

She took one last sweep of the ground floor, the soft glow of the overhead lighting coating everything in gentle gold, and turned back towards the door to the staff stairwell that would take her up to the new wing, where the meeting was due to start.

Two uniformed staff stood either side of the board-room doors and they greeted her with a small bow and shortly after she made her way to her seat the doors were closed. It always made her think of the phrase 'behind closed doors', of secrets and deals done in back rooms. And she hated that culture. Wanted it gone from the business that was as much a part of her as her family.

Finally, she forced herself to look at the man who wanted to blackmail her into stepping down from the vote. She wasn't surprised to find a smug grin and a knowing gleam in his eyes and for the first time she felt saddened by that, not angered. This man was also a member of her family—this man who had sold stories to the press about her, who had tried to push her and Nate aside so that he could reach for something that not only wasn't his by right, but by worth either. He just didn't deserve it. And if she hadn't already made up her mind, Hope thought that this realisation might have just swayed her.

Her grandfather stood from the head of the U-shaped wooden table and waited for silence to fall. Three rows of chairs behind each of the long wings of the table seated the entire number of board members and shareholders. The sense of heady expectation was thick in the air, most of the board darting frantic glances between her and Simon.

'Before we vote on the next CEO, is there any business to address?' her grandfather asked. Was she imagining the tone in his voice that made her think that Simon had warned him to expect her to step down? Or was it something else?

'I have something I need to bring to the table,' she said.

He gestured for her to proceed.

She stood, and almost instantly her legs nearly gave way. From the position of her chair, she'd not been able to see the rows at the back, and she hadn't even thought to look when she'd entered the room. She should have, though. Then she wouldn't have been so surprised to see not only her brother but Luca, standing right behind him, a mixture of thunderous frustration and admiration in his eyes, making her want to sob his name.

She hadn't wanted him here for so many reasons, but that he was, that he had somehow managed to get into this highly private and closely guarded business meeting meant the world to her. Apologies screamed from her silent lips and she could only hope that he might understand.

'Well?' Simon demanded, as if he had the right.

Refusing to give him even the courtesy of a glance, she faced her grandfather, the outgoing CEO and the CFO.

'Gentlemen,' she said, refusing to hide the emotion clogging her throat. 'Ladies,' she said, nodding to the hallowed few who had risen through the ranks. 'Before we get to the vote, I thought it would be good for you to know a little about me and Simon as people. You may think that because you've worked with us nearly all our adult lives,' she said, 'and knew us before that, even, you're aware of the kind of people we are. And it's possible that you do,' she admitted, shrugging. 'But, just in case you don't, I have something I'd like you to listen to.'

She removed her phone from her bag and tapped across the screen to pull up what she needed. To what she'd been able to record midway through the conversation which had taken place what felt almost like a lifetime ago.

Her voice broke into the silence from her phone. 'What do you want, Simon?'

'Let's not be coy about this. I know you have some kind of deal on the table in an attempt to woo the shareholders into voting for you in two days' time. But I doubt any deal would trump another sex scandal from you.'

'There hasn't even been one sex scandal.'

'Oh, I'm sure your ex-fiancé has something up his sleeve, if this doesn't do the trick. I want you to back out of the CEO vote, or I'll start digging.'

Simon stood up with such force it sent his chair falling back.

'This is outrageous,' he cried, increasing the volume of the disapproving muttering around her.

'No,' she said clearly, her voice loud enough to carry and quieten the voices of the shocked shareholders. 'What is outrageous is that you thought I would let you get away with attempting to blackmail me into giving up my desire to be Harcourts' next CEO. What is outrageous is that, once again, you—just like many others here—underestimated me terribly.

'And just in case anyone was wondering about the deal I have to woo you, let me explain. I have a signed deal with Sofia Obeid for the first of ten internationally located, exclusive luxury hotels to be branded Harcourts Obeid,' Hope said, pausing only long enough for that to sink in. 'They will be stocked with Harcourts' own brand and offer the ability to buy anything from the Harcourts' catalogue.' Excited whispers spread through the meeting. 'The revenue projections for the two-year mark,' she said, waiting to have everyone's attention, even Simon's, 'half a billion pounds.'

Now there was interest in the mix as well as excitement. She desperately wanted to look to her brother for confirmation, hating that she'd kept this from him, and hoping that he'd understand. Understand her need to have done this by herself, for herself. And then maybe, just maybe, Luca might too.

She turned to the head of the table, where she felt the weight of serious and heavy contemplation.

'I'm off the fence, Grandfather. I want the CEO position. So,' she said, turning back to the room, 'you can vote for someone who did absolutely nothing to forward Harcourts' interest and instead wanted to win by forcing out their opponent. Or you can vote for someone who refused to play games and instead made a business deal for your benefit. It's up to you,' she said, pushing back her chair and leaving the room without a backward glance.

Luca's heart was pounding so hard he was surprised it hadn't burst from his chest. He went to follow on her heels, and Nate held him back with surprising strength for someone who had needed a wheelchair to get to this room.

'Wait,' Nathanial Harcourt ordered.

'*Cazzo*, Nate—'

'Just wait. They need to see her leave. Alone. Powerful message.'

The truncated sentence concerned Luca and he looked back to the man beside him, who was beginning to sweat a little.

Luca cursed again. 'We should get you out of here,' he said, but Nate was staring off somewhere behind Luca. Turning around, he saw that the target of his fierce gaze was his grandfather. There was a nod between the two men before the Chairman of Harcourts broke the gaze and turned to his colleague.

'*Now* we go,' said Nate as they worked their way to

the side door, where some of Nate's assistants waited with the wheelchair to whisk him away from public sight before the meeting adjourned.

He waited long enough to see Nate settled, and after a glare and a, 'What are you waiting for?' from the other man, Luca rushed off in the direction he thought she'd gone.

Trusting his gut, he ran to the lifts and hit the call button, the doors parting instantly. He slammed his palm against the button for the ground floor, praying that Hope was doing the same just one or maybe two floors down. He held his breath and when the lift drew to a stop only moments after leaving the top floor, he knew he'd been right.

The doors parted and a startled Hope stared back at him. Before she could run away again, he reached for her wrist and pulled her into the lift with him and straight into an open-mouthed kiss.

It was punishment and pleasure; it was everything he couldn't say and everything he wanted to say. She gasped into his mouth and sagged against his body in willing submission, and everything in him roared in victory to have his hands on her again. He dragged himself back from the kiss only for enough time to hit the stop button, forcing a halt to the lift's progress.

A few seconds later, a voice came over the speaker. 'Is everything okay in there?'

'Yes,' Hope replied.

'Go away,' Luca commanded at the same time.

'Yes, ma'am, sir,' came the reply, as Luca let himself take the breath he'd not had since she'd flown away from him in Austria.

She pulled out of his hold, stepping back against the opposite side of the lift, her hands wrapping around the rail as if to stop herself reaching for him. Her eyes were full of hurt, shame and frustration.

'Nothing's changed, Luca.'

He shook his head slowly from side to side. Everything had changed, she just didn't know it yet. He wanted to prowl towards her, to press his body against hers until she melted against him again, but he knew they needed to speak first. There were things he needed to know and she needed to hear.

'Why didn't you tell me? About Simon?'

She bit her lip and clenched her jaw as if attempting to defy him and he wondered if she realised what hung in the balance here. But he was a patient man. He'd waited his entire life to meet her and he would wait for her to catch up, he would wait as long as it took her to realise that she loved him as much as he loved her.

She opened and closed her mouth and found her courage. 'My whole life people have been trying to protect me. My parents. Nate. You. Money made me a target, my gender made that easy. Simon's been undermining me as a way of getting to Nate for years. But all those things? They weren't about *me*,' she said, shrugging as if it hadn't hurt.

'People like Simon won't stop coming after me even if I do become CEO. So, are you and my brother going to find a way to protect me from every little threat I face? Or will you now finally trust that I can do this myself? That I have that power?' she demanded. 'I *needed* to do this by myself, to know that I could. Not for Simon, or the shareholders, or even you, but for *me*. I needed to know that I could do this.'

It nearly destroyed him that she hadn't known how strong she was. But he understood that need. The power of self-knowledge. Hadn't he felt it too when he'd confronted his mother?

'But now that I do know that, I realise that I don't have to,' she said softly, making him want to reach for her and pull her to him. It had been a terrible price for her to pay. Years of fighting to know herself. 'But that doesn't stop the threat of the news coming out about you and your mother. That hasn't changed, and I don't see how—'

He cut her words off with a kiss that he couldn't help any longer.

'Will you stop doing that?' she cried against his lips.

'No. Never. For the rest of our lives, if I think you are speaking utter nonsense, this is what will happen, just so you know,' he replied against her lips, though it was getting a little difficult to keep talking, kissing and smiling.

Hope pulled out of his hold, shock and hope pouring through her veins.

She stared up at him, cast in shadow by the emergency lighting, desperate to know what he'd meant by that. Questions he apparently read in her gaze.

'I went to see Anna,' he said, his use of her name telling.

Hope closed the distance between them, her hand reaching up to cup his jaw, to offer comfort and to be with him as he explained.

'She had been on my mind since we spoke and… she happened to be near to where I was already, so…' He shrugged but she saw the pain and the hurt that rippled across his features. 'I don't think she will ever be able to behave differently. Behave like a mother. Because she isn't one. Truly. I don't think she will ever be able to explain why she did what she did with the non-disclosure agreement. And for a moment there—I swear—I think she almost tried to blackmail me into silence again,' he admitted, the gravel in his voice dragging across her senses.

'Luca…' Hope said, his name conciliation on her tongue.

He shook his head. 'I protected her when I thought she needed it.'

'You protected her when she should have been protecting you,' Hope said gently, awareness flaring in her body when he locked his gaze on hers.

'Like you did,' he stated. 'You were never going to bow to Simon's threat, but you did it in such a way that he wouldn't have been able to reveal that threat without absolutely destroying himself in the eyes of his colleagues. You rendered his blackmail unusable. And I was that blackmail, wasn't I?' he demanded.

Hope looked away from the intensity in his eyes. She nodded, incapable of words at that point, her heart in her mouth. He was everything she'd wanted and more than she could have imagined and it was terrifying. A business wouldn't love her back, but he could. And she wanted it so much it made her sick.

'What did Martin say to you at the opera?' Luca asked. 'What did he say that you wanted?'

The question cut into her thoughts, spinning her back in time, and shame that he'd witnessed their encounter filled her again. She wanted to hide Martin's cruelty, but her loyalty and trust…they needed to be with Luca.

'Love. He said that I wanted love,' she admitted, tears pressing at the corners of her eyes.

Luca looked at her and she knew—she could feel his fury that her ex-fiancé had taunted her with such a thing—but she could also feel the need to give her that very same thing. She felt it shining from his eyes when he looked at her. She felt it in his touch when he held her.

And while she resented Martin for what he'd said, she knew, deep in her heart, that he'd been right. Beneath the mask and the facade she'd adopted to survive the loss of her parents, through boarding school, press attention and even working at Harcourts, had been a little girl just looking for someone to love her.

'You're ashamed of that?' Luca asked, his thumb under her chin, and a part of her was. A tear fell from her eye and he swept at it with his finger.

'Should I be ashamed of the same thing?' he asked

gently. 'For surely that was the only reason I protected Anna's secret.'

'What? No, of course not,' she said, outraged at the thought until realising the point he was making.

When he saw that she understood, he nodded. 'I love you. I love you so much that it is beyond me. I can't contain it. Marry me,' Luca asked against her lips.

Hope's tears fell into their kiss and were swept away by passion and promises, and she felt as if something had finally slotted into place to make her complete. As if the world had been righted on its axis when she hadn't known it was off-kilter. And now she knew the power of what it was to love and be loved. This amazing, proud, powerful man would stand by her and support whatever she did, just as she would him, and she knew that as well as she knew the sky was blue and the earth was round.

'I don't have fancy words, but I have a declaration for you. You will never have to ask, or wonder, or doubt again. I know your name,' Luca said, his voice a whisper and a quote she recognised from Turandot, the opera they had seen that night, her heart flaring at his words. 'I know your name,' he repeated. 'Your name is love.'

Overwhelmed by the love she felt from him, by the love she felt for him, she could only say, 'Yes. Yes, yes, yes...' over and over again until she believed it. Until she knew that she was going to spend the rest of her life loving and being loved by Luca Calvino.

'Erm, sorry to interrupt, ma'am.'

Hope waved an arm as if trying to get rid of the voice.

'We're going to have to start the lift up again, ma'am.'

The floor beneath Hope jerked into action just a moment later.

'And ma'am? The shareholders' vote just came in. May I be the first to congratulate our new CEO?'

Luca wrenched his lips from hers long enough to look at her in a way that told her so much. Love, pride, excitement, desire…and then went right back to kissing her socks off. And when the lift doors opened and the press caught sight of them, so wrapped up in each other they couldn't even stop kissing, they went wild and Hope and Luca didn't care one bit. They were done hiding their love.

EPILOGUE

LUCA LEANED BACK in his chair, making sure that the shade of the pergola covered both him and his daughter, fast asleep on his chest. He felt her cheek with the back of his hand, making sure that she wasn't too hot beneath the Italian sun, his concern easing when he found Felicity's skin warm but not hot. Even at four months old, his second daughter was far too much like her mother—refusing to complain or demand help when she needed it.

The papoose fit her snugly against him and he was sure he'd never tire of the feeling. He certainly hadn't with Bella, their first daughter, who—at the age of four—was ordering her twin cousins around the garden like a general.

'Gabbi, you should tell her to stop if she's too much,' he said to his sister-in-law, who was watching the three children from the seat beside him. They were playing out in the early summer sun in the sprawling garden that had become the cornerstone of Luca's heart and home.

Gabbi Casas waved him off with a sweep of her

hand. 'It's wonderful to see. The twins need to be kept on their toes or they'll really start to believe that they rule over everything.'

Luca smiled. The twins were a rambunctious pair and the absolute love of their parents' lives—and they did rule over everything. He looked over to where his wife and her own twin brother were head-to-head over a small table between them, a fierce chess game taking all their concentration. What had started as a way to keep Nate's healing brain active and nimble had become deeply enmeshed in the siblings' relationship.

'I'm so glad she can play him. He just wins every time with me.'

'Don't try and pull that with me,' Luca said, laughing, 'I know that you let him win.'

Gabbi's face turned towards him, the blank expression making him laugh even more, and he struggled not to wake Felicity.

'You're secretly a chess master, aren't you?' he demanded.

'Only in my spare time, but don't tell Nate that.'

Luca's cheeks hurt from the happiness he felt here. This was his home. It was full of laughter and love and fun and ease. No, his marriage to Hope hadn't all been smiles. It had been a hard road to navigate as Hope struggled with the pressures of her job, and then with infertility issues—the fear and self-doubt that had come with that. Had she waited too long? Had she sacrificed too much for Harcourts? Luca shook his head, remembering the shock and the pain of those years. Thankfully, after only two rounds of IVF, Bella had come into their lives and Luca and Hope had thought their lives complete. And then, out of the blue, just a little over four years later, Felicity came along, determined to make everyone sit up and notice.

Looking back on his own childhood, Luca could never have imagined the sheer light that he lived in now. They had navigated—and survived—the fallout from the press linking him to Anna Bertoli, which they all suspected had been Simon's last jab after losing the vote for CEO before he'd retired to the world of private investment. Anna had pivoted the initial few days of very painful and public backlash against her into something positive as she became an ambassador for a single parents' charity and, despite fears, managed a number one box office hit in the wake of the attention. And while he and his mother had a strained relationship, the love that Hope and their children had brought into his life made it much easier to bear.

Hope had done incredible things with Harcourts. The deal with Sofia Obeid had been a roaring success, to the point where it was rolled out globally and had also led to another partnership of a different kind. Hope, Gabbi and Sofia had joined forces to create a small but hugely successful fashion brand, after launching three collections, male, female and non-binary. Gabbi ran the day-to-day business but it was a joint effort that each of the women loved. In the meantime, Harcourts had produced more accessible

and specific lines for each department store's local
community. It worked slightly differently to the rest
of the store, but the small and often rotated stock and
start-up brands regularly drew a lot of interest and
support, selling out just as much as the more exclusive brands and designers.

'Hope, sunscreen!' he called out to his wife.

'The kids are fine,' Hope said, without raising her
attention from the chessboard between her and her
brother.

'I meant for you,' Luca shouted back.

Nate laughed.

'That goes for you too, husband,' chided Gabbi.

'It's okay for you two with your Mediterranean
colouring,' Nate groused.

'Yeah, well, we can't all have been in a hospital
for nearly two years,' Luca teased.

It was one of the things that Hope loved most about
the relationship between her brother and her husband.
They'd had it from the very start—a way of communicating that was as much a brotherly bond as Hope
could imagine. She'd not realised how worried she'd
been that they wouldn't get on until it came time to
reintroduce Luca to Nate as her fiancé. She'd wanted
more than civility, not only for herself but for Luca
who deserved a huge, sprawling, loud, messy, cha-
otic family so different from the cold loneliness and
rejection he'd had growing up. But she needn't have
worried. The men were fast friends and firm in their

loyalty and love. Which was pretty much the way she felt about Gabbi.

When she'd learned of the beginning of their relationship, she'd felt acutely aware that she had played an accidental part in keeping them apart, feeling as if she'd still needed to protect Nate's privacy back then. But at least and at last, they'd found their way back to each other and with a happiness that maybe matched—but not rivalled—her own. She looked back to the large wooden table beneath the pergola that looked out across the Italian hillside.

They spent every holiday possible at their villa in Tuscany and last year their grandfather had even come out. Interactions had been slightly stilted, but Hope had loved having all the generations in the house together. Usually, the big family occasions were Nate's family and hers, together all under the one roof, and Hope nearly had to pinch herself. Remembering the time when she had nearly lost her brother, and then when she had nearly let such an incredible man—Luca—slip through her fingers, it didn't bear thinking about. Goosebumps raised on her skin briefly as she applied the sunscreen as prompted by her husband.

For all her focus on the Harcourts CEO position back then, Sofia had been right. Harcourts the department store would never love her back. But the family? Her family? What she had made of it—even after being so scared to even hope what it could be—was everything. It hadn't always been easy—Luca was still commanding and demanding, and she was still stubborn and occasionally—*occasionally*—worked too hard. But it was hers, and the love she felt, it grew even more each and every day. She'd once thought that love had a capacity, a certain amount that could be given or received, but her husband and daughters showed her that, actually, the capacity for love was infinite, and it was a lesson she loved learning over and over again each day for the rest of her life.

* * * * *

Did In Bed with Her Billionaire Bodyguard
leave you wanting more?
Then don't miss these other stories
by Pippa Roscoe!

Stolen from Her Royal Wedding
Claimed to Save His Crown
The Wife the Spaniard Never Forgot
Expecting Her Enemy's Heir
His Jet-Set Nights with the Innocent

Available now!

#4169 THE BABY HIS SECRETARY CARRIES
Bound by a Surrogate Baby
by Dani Collins
Faced with a hostile takeover, tycoon Gio must strengthen his claim on the Casella family company with a fake engagement. He'll never commit to a real one again. Despite his forbidden attraction, his dedicated PA, Molly, is ideal to play his adoring fiancée. The only problem? Molly's pregnant!

#4170 THE ITALIAN'S PREGNANT ENEMY
A Diamond in the Rough
by Maisey Yates
Billionaire Dario's electric night with his mentor's daughter Lyssia was already out-of-bounds. But six weeks later, she drops the bombshell that she's pregnant! Growing up on the streets of Rome, Dario fought for his safety, and he is determined to make his child equally safe. There is just one solution—marrying his enemy!

#4171 WEDDING NIGHT IN THE KING'S BED
by Caitlin Crews
Innocent Helene is unprepared for the wildfire that awakens at the sight of her convenient husband, King Gianluca San Felice. And she is undone by the craving that consumes them on their wedding night. But outside the royal bedchamber, Gianluca remains ice-cold—dare Helene believe their chemistry is enough to bring this powerful ruler to his knees?

#4172 THE BUMP IN THEIR FORBIDDEN REUNION
The Fast Track Billionaires' Club
by Amanda Cinelli
Former race car driver Grayson crashes Izzy's fertility appointment to reveal his late best friend's deceit before it's too late. He always desired Izzy, but their reunion unlocks something primal in Grayson. Knowing she feels it too compels the cynical billionaire to make a scandalous offer: *he'll* give her the family she wants!

HPCNMRA1223

#4173 HIS LAST-MINUTE DESERT QUEEN
by Annie West
Determined to save her cousin from an unwanted marriage, Miranda daringly kidnaps the groom-to-be, Sheikh Zamir. She didn't expect him to turn the tables and demand she become his queen instead—and now, he has all the power...

#4174 A VOW TO REDEEM THE GREEK
by Jackie Ashenden
The dying wish of Elena's adoptive father is to be reunited with his estranged son, Atticus. Whatever it takes, she must track down the reclusive billionaire. When she finally finds him, she's completely unprepared for the wildfire raging between them. Or for his father's unexpected demand that they marry!

#4175 AN INNOCENT'S DEAL WITH THE DEVIL
Billion-Dollar Fairy Tales
by Tara Pammi
When Yana Reddy's former stepbrother walks back into her life, his outrageous offer has her playing with fire! Nasir Hadeed will clear all her debts *if* she helps look after his daughter for three months. It's a dangerous deal—she's been burned by him before, and he remains the innocent's greatest temptation...

#4176 PLAYING THE SICILIAN'S GAME OF REVENGE
by Lorraine Hall
When Saverina Parisi discovers her engagement is part of fiancé Teo LaRosa's ruthless vendetta against her family's empire, her hurt is matched only by her need to destroy the same enemy. She'll play along and take pleasure in testing his patience. But Saverina doesn't expect their burning connection to evolve into so much more...

YOU CAN FIND MORE INFORMATION ON UPCOMING HARLEQUIN TITLES, FREE EXCERPTS AND MORE AT HARLEQUIN.COM.

HPCNMRB1223

Get 3 FREE REWARDS!

We'll send you 2 FREE Books plus a FREE Mystery Gift.

FREE Value Over **$20**

Both the **Harlequin® Desire** and **Harlequin Presents®** series feature compelling novels filled with passion, sensuality and intriguing scandals.